Advanced Praise for

The Seasons of Wick's Content

Ron Johnston guides us through a man's journey of self-discovery and self-awareness, a dream-inspired tale full of wistful nostalgia, meaningful relationships, hopeful optimism, and basic human decency. What a refreshing alternative to prevailing cultural trends of crudeness and cynicism! Readers will be endeared to Wick's earnest personal growth, and challenged to seek similar flourishing in their own lives.

—Dale McConkey, Ph.D., Associate Professor of Sociology and Chair of Sociology and Anthropology, Berry College, Mount Berry, GA

Ron Johnston showed his potential as a writer 50 years ago when I gave him his first byline in the newspaper business, so it is not a surprise to me that his first book is an interesting read. Anyone who came of age in the 60's and 70's will identify with Wick Watters and the sometimes winding path he takes to turn his writing skills into a successful career. Although not always apparent at the time, Wick usually manages to find himself at the right place at the right time, enabling Ron to engage the reader in an enjoyable ride as he and Wick join a long line of successful writers who got their start in a newspaper Sports department.

—Henry Freeman, founding Sports Editor, *USA TODAY*

Johnston's debut novel is a poignant tour through the landmarks and the people that make the South—and its newspapers—memorable. The Northwest Georgia foothills and their rich Native American history are depicted eloquently alongside my beloved Rome News-Tribune. The book's theme of contentment, even during struggle, will resonate with anyone who has invested themselves in building family, friendships and career over a lifetime.

—Elizabeth Crumbly, freelance writer, *Atlanta Journal-Constitution* and *Rome News-Tribune*

The Seasons of Wick's Content

To: Bethany

May you always be content.

Ron Johnson
12/20/24

To: Bethany

May you always be content.

The Seasons of Wick's Content

Ron Johnston

JOHNSTON MEDIA
CONSORT

Copyright © 2023 Charles Ronald Johnston

No part of this publication may be reproduced, stored or introduced into a retrieval system or transmitted, in any form, or by any means (electronic, photocopying, recording, or otherwise), without the prior written permission of both the copyright owner and the above publisher of this book.

For information about permission to reproduce selections from this book:

Email: jcronald72@gmail.com Please put Permissions in the subject line.
Published in the USA by Johnston Media Consort

JOHNSTON MEDIA CONSORT

Publisher's Cataloging-in-Publication (Provided by Cassidy Cataloguing Services, Inc.)
Names: Johnston, Charles Ronald, 1950– author.
Title: The seasons of Wick's content / Ron Johnston.
Description: [Braselton, Georgia] : Johnston Media Consort, [2023] Identifiers: ISBN: 979-8-218-19004-0 (trade paperback) | 979-8-218-19003-3 (ebook) | LCCN: 2023936316
Subjects: LCSH: Authors, American—Fiction. | Friendship—Fiction. | Cherokee Indians—Fiction. | Families—History—Fiction. | Food industry and trade—United States—Fiction. | Southern States—Social life and customs—Fiction. | World War, 1939-1945—Naval operations, American—Fiction. | Military training camps—United States—Fiction. | Dogs—Fiction. | Parents—Death—Psychological aspects—Fiction. | Sister—Death—Psychological aspects—Fiction. | LCGFT: Historical fiction. | Nonfiction novels. | BISAC: FICTION / Historical / 20th Century / General. | BIOGRAPHY & AUTOBIOGRAPHY / General. | BIOGRAPHY & AUTOBIOGRAPHY / Editors, Journalists, Publishers.
Classification: LCC: PS3610.O3843 S43 2023 | DDC: 813/.6—dc23

Dedicated to . . .

Harriet, for making me a better man

Erin and Russell, for sharing Sage

Bob and Blossom, for enabling my dream

Contents

Introduction	1
CHAPTER 1: What's in a Name?	3
CHAPTER 2: Uncle Sam	9
CHAPTER 3: Half & Half	12
CHAPTER 4: The Last Straw	16
CHAPTER 5: True Grit	19
CHAPTER 6: When in Rome	23
CHAPTER 7: Uncle Tom	28
CHAPTER 8: Anchored in Alaska	33
CHAPTER 9: Bahama Blue	37
CHAPTER 10: Scarlet Letter	48
CHAPTER 11: Delta Epsilon	52
CHAPTER 12: Redemption	64
CHAPTER 13: Greenville	67
CHAPTER 14: Legends	77
CHAPTER 15: Fort Knox	86
CHAPTER 16: Oostanaula Vows	99
CHAPTER 17: Lewis	110
CHAPTER 18: Catfish	122
CHAPTER 19: Sequoyah's Spirits	125
CHAPTER 20: Frequent Flyer	142
CHAPTER 21: Johnny Harris	167
CHAPTER 22: Playlist	185
CHAPTER 23: Pamplona	189
CHAPTER 24: Sage	200
CHAPTER 25: Still Watters	212
CHAPTER 26: Welcome Back	229
Acknowledgments	231
About the Author	235

Introduction

Did you ever dream a story all in one night? A complete story in full color, covering decades, with seasons of stories and episodes running the full range of emotions?

I did.

About a man named Wick on his way to a writing career, and the people, places, and events that shape his life. Classmate Hollie O'Hara figures prominently into his quest, as does the familial character Tom Prophett, a Cherokee Indian who becomes Wick's rock. The man's integrity, wisdom, love, and loyalty guide Wick when he needs it most. Prophett's influence is always there, even when the omniscient Cherokee isn't.

Contentment, in its different manifestations, can steer one's life in the direction one desires. The best prescription for happiness is not found in a bottle nor in one's bank account. Instead, it's how you respond when you stop to take a look at the world around you. Contentment is finding solace in the simple things that make a person smile, laugh, love, and share; and never, *ever* taking for granted the blessings of good friends.

Wick didn't.

His journey begins here, with a few flashbacks along the way for history, context, and perspective.

I'll see you again at the end of the dream . . .

Chapter One

What's in a Name?

He was born smack dab in the middle of the twentieth century on January 1, 1950, but the life of Coleman Brunswick Watters was anything but middle of the road.

Harry Truman was still in the White House, though he would forego a second campaign for the presidency, having served all but three months of Franklin Roosevelt's fourth term. FDR, in failing health near the end of an already unprecedented third term, willed himself through the political season to win the office yet again, but died April 12, 1945, in the "Little White House" just down the road in Warm Springs, Georgia.

Truman had shocked the pundits and most of America for his first elected term in 1948 by defeating Thomas Dewey, the heavily favored former governor of New York. The battle cry from Truman loyalists had been "Give 'em hell, Harry," and he did.

Harry "S" Truman was the only US president without a middle name. The middle initial reportedly was a compromise to satisfy his two grandfathers who had names beginning with the letter.

This nugget of presidential trivia resonated with young Watters every time his schoolteachers called their rolls. He indeed had a full name but did not go by his first name, Coleman, nor the shortened "Cole."

It seemed only appropriate for Reed and Rose Watters, proud grandparents and owners of their new stew business, to recommend "Brunswick" for the newest grandson's middle moniker. This was not to honor any legacy or lineage but to acknowledge and celebrate their new family enterprise, "Uncle Tom's Famous Brunswick Stew."

The suggestion was well received by the new parents, Reed and Rose's youngest son Raleigh and wife Edith. While Brunswick was intended to be the name by which he would be called, young Watters's name was spontaneously shortened to "Wick" by a mellow and merlot-inspired Aunt Katie upon his arrival home from the hospital. The nickname stuck from that day forward like simmering stew to the bottom of an unstirred kettle.

The Watters family—more specifically Reed—was well endowed with male chromosomes. Over fourteen years, from 1911 to 1925, Rose gave birth to seven boys: Albert, Reed Jr., Richard, Burton, Will, Harry, and Raleigh. Rose, a talented seamstress, made and mended many a boy's shirt, pants, and coat during the Great Depression, and also stayed busy tailoring both men's and women's clothing for the well-to-do families around Rome, Georgia, where the family lived. And she did it all while Iggy, her faithful Scottish fold feline, lay content on the leaf of her Singer treadle as Rose pedaled away.

The late '20s and '30s were lean years for sure. Wick remembered his father, youngest of the seven boys, saying, "I was thirteen before I put on a pair of pants and shirt that someone else hadn't worn before me."

Reed "Papa" Watters—Raleigh's father and Wick's grandfather—was born in July 1888, barely one generation after the Civil War, and Reed's father, Monroe, in 1858, only three years before its beginning. Understandably, Raleigh and his older brothers had plenty of stories to pass down to young Wick, his siblings, and their cousins. Rose Morrison, born one month after Reed in August 1888, became girlfriend, fiancée, wife, mother, and grandmother, hearing and living many of those stories for the rest of her rich life.

Reed was a fast learner, whether at work or in school. And he had to be. His parents, Monroe and Audrey Watters, had nine children, and as the oldest of the four sons, Reed found himself at sixteen growing up even faster when his father died unexpectedly at only forty-six; his mother needed to lean on him more than ever. Reed fully assumed the responsibility, always there for his brothers and sisters, and certainly for his mom. Audrey lived to ninety-five, with Reed receiving a deferment during World War I as the sole provider for his own growing family, which included Miss Audrey.

The same year his father passed, 1905, Reed was among twenty-four charter enrollees in the new Darlington School, destined to become one of the South's elite preparatory schools. With their new building not yet ready for occupancy, the first day of class on September 11 was spartan but thankfully satisfactory. The room above the Rome Fire Station served as the lone classroom for Dr. James Ross McCain's pupils. Without a blackboard or desks, and only chairs to seat and teach multiple grades, McCain somehow made it all work.

As time went on, Reed hungered for more experiential lessons and less academia. Though a good student, he was anxious to get on with some enterprise that would transform him into a merchant. His late father an established grocer, Reed had on many occasions accompanied his dad to the "Cotton Block," Rome's equivalent to Wall Street. In those days, virtually any buying or selling in town happened here. As the name suggests, cotton was the lead commodity procured in the busy space off Broad Street and between First and Second Avenues. However, the Cotton Block became much more—a venue to buy/sell/trade whatever one could deal to the public, from fabric to hard goods to livestock. All the transactions represented commerce, and the activity beckoned Reed Watters.

After finishing Darlington, and before he would become a regular at the Cotton Block, young Reed used his skills as a self-taught carpenter to land a job building barracks at Fort Oglethorpe, situated along the state line of northern Georgia and southeast Tennessee. Though his "sole provider" status excused him from serving in The Great War, this carpentry opportunity allowed him to serve his country in another way. Begun as an army post for the Sixth Cavalry in 1904, Fort Oglethorpe would become home for some four thousand German prisoners of war and civilian detainees during World War I.

As time progressed, Reed found himself gravitating to the Cotton Block more and more, listening and learning from the best dealers around while formulating his own pitch for when his time came to register with the market's chief procurement officer. In the meantime, the industrious Reed opened a restaurant that became the most successful one in north Rome. The "Wattering Whole" featured a wide menu; its barbequed pork sandwich with an iced cold Schlitz topped off with a slice of homemade coconut cream pie was the most popular.

Leveraging his father's legacy in the grocery business, Reed tapped into long-standing relationships and also found success in buying and selling livestock. Pigs, cows, horses, mules, goats, sheep—if it walked on four legs, Reed Watters had a deal for you. This experience propelled him into a higher status among peers in the Cotton Block, but that status might have come into question if the story of Reed and the ox, many years later, would have become public knowledge. The incident happened in the midst of a light rainfall when Reed and his sons Albert, Reed Jr., and Burton were trying to coerce a steer onto their flatbed truck.

The pulling and tugging by all four men simply wasn't working, until Reed Jr. had the idea to wire a cattle prod to the truck battery. On a cue from junior, Reed was to grab the beefy bullock by the horns and pull forward toward the truck cab. Whether Reed Jr. knew exactly what he was doing or not, he hollered, "NOW!" while positioning the prod in the most efficient spot on the stubborn steer. As soon as senior gripped the horns, sparks shot out of both ends of the animal's horns, and the electric shock propelled Reed upward and back on top of the truck cab. After immediately jumping onto the bed to determine their father was okay, laughter rang out from the Watters boys. Papa Watters was not laughing, however. He was busy evoking every expletive in his repertoire.

The boys liked to recount stories involving "Uncle Bud," one of Reed's older brothers. And Wick loved to listen, no matter how many times the stories were told.

Uncle Bud and his signature corncob pipe were inseparable. He kept it clenched between his teeth, which made his speech difficult to understand at times. He wasn't a fast talker either, so one really had to hear the full measure of his words to stitch his message together.

One day, Reed had an errand to run over at the Rome Feed &

Seed, and he asked Uncle Bud if he would like to hop on for the ride—driving the same flatbed truck from the shocked steer anecdote. He did, and it was an easy hop, as the old truck was missing both doors. One had been torn off when one of the boys was backing into a warehouse but did not realize the passenger door was hanging open. The same happened to the driver door when Reed once left the parking brake off and the truck rolled back, swiping a huge sawtooth oak.

Reed was waiting to pull out onto old Martha Berry Highway and turn left to head into town. Reed could see his side was clear and, without turning his head, said, "Anything coming, Bud?"

Following a brief pause, Uncle Bud began, "Nothing . . . coming . . . but . . . a . . . yellow . . . truck."

By the time Reed heard "nothing," he was already halfway in the road. When he heard a blaring horn, he glanced over his shoulder and saw a bigger truck barreling down on them. He mashed the gas pedal to the floor and barely made the turn as he straddled the right side of the road to get out of the way. When the yellow tornado had passed, Reed checked to his right to see if Uncle Bud was okay. He did a double take because Uncle Bud wasn't there. Reed immediately turned around and looked back through the cab window to see two legs pointed up out of the ditch. He jumped out of the cab and ran frantically down the road, yelling, "Bud, Bud, are you okay?" When Reed arrived, Uncle Bud was dusted up a little, but the pipe was still clenched between his teeth.

"Damn . . . Reed . . . didn't . . . you . . . hear . . . me?"

Needless to say, Reed never relied on Uncle Bud's navigation again.

Chapter Two

Uncle Sam

Reed was understandably proud of his family and of each son, all serving their country in some capacity during World War II.

Albert, the oldest, served under General George S. Patton as a captain in the Signal Corps. As the Third Army advanced through France and Germany, Albert was confronted with an insurgence that would call on every instinct in his body and mind. The Signal Corps mission was to run and repair all communication lines between command headquarters and the general. Most importantly, Patton had received intelligence from the field that German officers were using civilians to climb the telephone poles at nighttime to cut phone lines. Patton's orders were crystal clear: Shoot on sight. No exceptions. Communications were that critical on the Third Army's march to Berlin.

There was plenty of snow on the ground from earlier that bitterly cold winter day. In the faint moonlight Albert spotted a figure climbing fast and ever closer to the top of a targeted pole, wire cutters in hand. Albert's arms quaked as he drew the figure into the crosshairs of his rifle scope. The moon offered enough light on this clear night to discern that this was no enemy soldier. Was this a young man?

"My God, this is a boy," Albert whispered to himself.

You do not and cannot disobey orders, especially Patton's, he reconciled. Slowly, Albert steadied his aim. Just as the trespasser positioned the cutters in his right hand while hanging onto the other lines with his left for balance, Captain Albert Watters squeezed the trigger and life right out of a scared but compliant blond-headed child. The boy slid about twenty feet down the pole, taut arms embracing it until both fell limp, releasing his body to collapse upon the frozen footprints he had made in the snow only moments before. The boy couldn't have been more than thirteen or fourteen.

The incident became a nightmare that invaded Albert's dreams from that night forward, following him all the way back to Rome. He told himself that being back home with his family would somehow mitigate the horrors of war, but it never did.

Fortunately for Reed and Rose, Albert was the only son who had to kill during the war, but the fact it had been a boy magnified the painful memory for the Watters family.

Reed Jr. somehow made his way to Haiti to run a hemp plantation. Wick later remembered seeing an 8 x 10 black-and-white glossy of Uncle Reed in a Panama hat, dressed in all-white pants and shirt, sitting atop a white horse. Hemp fiber production was necessary during the war to make ropes for the US Navy. Ironically, youngest brother Raleigh was in the navy at the same time when his troop transport ship made a stop in Port-au-Prince for supplies. He had no idea brother Reed was on the island. Personal communications—both letters and phone calls—were constrained during the war.

Richard, living in Nashville, worked for a Jeep manufacturing plant that contracted with the Department of Defense to build transport vehicles of varying sizes and specs for the US Army.

Burton, who had an uncanny ability to disassemble virtually anything mechanical and return it to its original construct was lured to Birmingham by a manufacturer of airplane engines.

Will served in the US Army infantry, with assignments in England and France. With more time invested in France, the handsome soldier came back with a good grasp of the French language and an affinity for fine Bordeaux.

Harry graduated the US Military Academy in 1945 with a degree in biological sciences. From West Point he was assigned to Walter Reed General Hospital in DC, focusing on epidemiology.

Raleigh was itching to join the war. All his friends were older and already in the service. He once told son Wick, "I turned around and all my friends were gone." Raleigh was certain he would be drafted, especially after the attack on Pearl Harbor. He waited and wondered when the mailman would bring a "Greetings" letter from Uncle Sam. Years later he speculated that Papa Watters, a friend of the draft board director, had asked a favor to move Raleigh's file to the back of the drawer.

Chapter Three

Half & Half

Tired of waiting, down to the local recruiter's office went Raleigh. He was ready to join.

"You can't," said the recruiting officer after looking into his updated files. "I'm showing you're already registered for the draft, so I can't enlist you here. Go down to the induction center and tell them you are appearing as a volunteer inductee."

Raleigh went straight there, repeating his story to the receptionist. She directed him to follow the hall to the open door at the end where he would see several tables. When he stepped into the room, he saw a table for each branch—Army, Navy, Marine Corps, Coast Guard, and National Guard.

He froze for a moment, finding himself the only candidate in the room. Each uniformed officer, replete in their regalia, appeared imposing behind their appointed tables and stacks of brochures. "Come over here, son" or "Give us a look-see," called out each rep in one form or another.

Raleigh continued to pause, until the navy officer held up his right hand and motioned with his index finger for Raleigh to walk his way. "Wouldn't you rather ride than walk, young man?"

It must have been his memories of all those summers swimming downtown in the Etowah and Oostanaula rivers that persuaded Raleigh to oblige. By November of 1943 he was on his way to boot camp at Great Lakes Navy Base about an hour north of Chicago.

During boot camp Raleigh consistently excelled on the shooting range. He was disappointed, however, when his deployment papers did not include an assignment with the fleet. Because of his sharp eye and accuracy, Raleigh was designated for the Naval Armed Guard, which meant he would join a select group of sharpshooters with exceptional skills in manning the navy's 30mm artillery cannon. His group was assigned to a variety of ships, from troop transports to oil tankers. They were there to protect their cargo, whether sailors or soldiers, critical oil or equipment. As it turned out, Raleigh saw more of the world on these assignments than he would have if attached to the fleet or only one ship.

His tours included two through the Panama Canal; the Middle East, especially those ports within the Persian Gulf; and Australia. His ship was on the way to Japan when the captain received word the "War Is Over," with orders to turn the ship around and head back to the States, San Francisco specifically. Though dejected they would not make it to Tokyo, Raleigh was indeed elated Japan had surrendered. Truman's decision to drop two atomic bombs had brought the Pacific war to an end.

One of Wick's favorite stories of his father was about his Australian trip to Sydney and Brisbane.

After a week in port at Sydney, Raleigh and five of his shipmates ventured out on weekend leave to head into downtown. It was as big a city as any of them had seen thus far, and they tried enthusiastically to see it all. By the time all had a bite of dinner, they decided to head out toward the countryside. From there they wandered and found a local tavern that more than one person had recommended. PJ Tilly's, they were told, had the best brews, especially the half & half (pronounced *'off n 'off* in Australian).

The special "cocktail" was actually half pale ale and half stout, and the six sailors had well more than half. As the night wore on and they were making their way back to the ship, one of the navy's best suggested they were ahead of schedule, and one more half & half for the road sure would taste good. Fact was, they were all more than sufficiently inebriated already, but somehow they wobbled their way back to PJ Tilly's.

When the lively group arrived, the tavern lights were out and the door locked, which was not unusual being that it was three thirty a.m. This establishment was a quaint stone two-story with copper awnings and Tudor-style vertical swing windows, a typical independent business format with the tavern downstairs and proprietor's living quarters upstairs. Not to be deterred, a couple of the sailors began pounding on the huge, thick wooden door. After about two minutes, a light came on in the window directly above same door. The anxious repeat customers smiled, sure they would soon be having one more half & half.

The two glass windows swung open as the owner leaned out and peered down. He recognized the motley crew right away, his nightcap and gown waving in the gentle breeze. "My God, mates. What is it you want? It's three something in the bloody morning!"

"Might we trouble you, sir, for one more half & half before we head back to port?" the bravest of the drunken sailors asked.

"Wait right there, boys." The tavern owner smiled.

The six stood pat in front of the door, mistakenly thinking the cooperative proprietor was coming down to let them in.

Instead, he appeared again in the window with a bedpan, pouring down its contents with remarkable accuracy.

"There you go, mates. That's 'off mine and 'off the misses'."

Soaked now with more than alcohol, the outsmarted sailors made their way back toward the railroad tracks, finding a coal car that was rolling its way to the Sydney port before time ran out on their curfew.

Chapter Four

The Last Straw

When Raleigh's ship arrived in San Francisco, he was assigned to Treasure Island until his separation papers arrived. For three weeks he worked in the navy's supply warehouse, filling requisitions for officers and personnel in the Bay area. Then he bought his ticket for a three-day cross-country train ride to Atlanta, and a bus ride on to Rome.

He stayed in Rome for almost a year, doing jobs around the house and farm for Reed and Rose. But he became restless and bored, and decided he would head back to San Francisco to reenlist. This time maybe he would apply for training in one of the navy's internal security platoons.

Before he left, he strolled into Vick's, a popular diner and soda fountain in Rome next to the DeSoto theatre, on a Saturday afternoon. Maybe he would catch a movie if they had a good Tom Mix or Gene Autry picture playing.

A troubled young lady left the booth where a boy who

had obviously been drinking was harassing her. She chose one of the padded counter stools about six down from where Raleigh sat siphoning one of Vick's signature chocolate malts through his paper straw. Her sniffles and crying became more audible, which prompted him to crane his neck to see the distraught lady for himself. She was now slightly slumped over the counter.

Raleigh had seen enough. He picked up his malt and approached the young woman, sitting on the stool to her left.

"Excuse me, miss. I don't mean to be nosy, but I could see you are upset. Is there anything I can do to help you?"

She turned slowly toward him, wiping her eyes; still wet with tears, they were sparkling, brown, and beautiful. She had a cute nose and mouth too, but she had been wounded with words.

"That boy in the third booth scares me. He's been drinking and is saying awful things to me. I was afraid to go out the door to leave. Terrified he might follow me."

"You're safe now. Just sit right there. I'll be back in a couple minutes," Raleigh assured her, responding to the classic damsel in distress.

He meandered slowly to the booth where the problem sat, seated himself, and looked the guy straight in the eyes.

"My name is Raleigh Watters. It doesn't really matter what yours is. The little lady at the counter has been crying because you said some ugly things to her. And it's obvious you've had too much to drink. I can escort you to the door and around the corner to the alley behind this building, or you can get up and walk out on your own. Either option is fine with me. Just don't come back when I or the lady are here."

Without a word, the sobering boy eased out of his seat, stood up, and walked out.

The lady at the counter had calmed down now. She felt safe, and on February 25, 1947, Edith Beamish would wed Raleigh Watters and stay safe for the next fifty-seven years.

Chapter Five

True Grit

Much like his grandfather, young Wick was restless to do something, build something. He enjoyed school and was a good student, but at thirteen he was anxious to find a part-time job. He yearned to be outside of the classroom, outside the house, engaging with people.

He was spending some weekends at Papa and Momma Watters' home on North Broad Street, not far from the canning plant. A number of businesses within four blocks either way were possibilities.

Jennings Funeral Home sat across the street. Convenient, but not exactly appealing to a young teen. Wick preferred to be around live people. Three blocks north of his grandparents' house was Rowe's Supermarket, which coincidentally was the first grocery store to stock Uncle Tom's Brunswick Stew, canned by Wick's grandparents. As a result, Herbert Rowe and Papa had become good friends. Wick swung his right leg over his red-and-black Schwinn bike and pedaled up to Rowe's.

When Wick asked to see Mr. Rowe, one of the bag boys pointed to the small, elevated office at the front left corner. Herbert had heard the youthful voice and pushed up from his chair to crane above the short privacy wall. He stood only five foot seven, about the same height as Wick.

"Aren't you Reed Watters's grandson?" he said to the eager boy.

"Yes, sir, I am," Wick answered with a clear voice and firm handshake. Papa had instilled in him the importance of both when introducing one's self to an adult.

"Your grandfather's a good man. What can I do for you today?"

"Do you happen to have any openings, Mr. Rowe? I'm looking for a part-time job."

"Well," hesitated Herbert as he pushed his eyeglasses farther up his nose with his index finger, "you're not old enough to run a register, and you're really not big enough to handle one of these tall carts we have to roll off the curb when taking groceries to a customer's car. Unfortunately, I'm carrying more bag boys than I need right now."

Wick was deflated, but he understood and thanked Mr. Rowe for his time.

"Come back to me in a year when you've grown more and let's talk about a job then. In the meantime, please tell your grandfather I said hello."

"I sure will, Mr. Rowe," waved Wick as he walked out the door, determined to find a job somewhere. After a couple other inquiries at the gas station and car wash yielded the same results, he pedaled back to his grandparents' house. When Papa arrived home that Friday evening, Wick told them about his conversation with Mr. Rowe.

"I admire your initiative, Wick, but I'm sure Herbert is honest about why he couldn't hire you right now, even if he had an opening."

A few days later, Reed would drop in to thank his friend for leaving the door open for his ambitious grandson. Reed could have, of course, put Wick to work at the canning plant, sweeping, mopping, breaking down boxes, or some other tasks, but he wanted his grandson to experience the thrill of finding his first job all on his own.

As was customary after dinner, Papa sat down in his easy chair to read the *Rome News Tribune* while Mama Watters, seated across the room, enjoyed her favorite publication.

Holding up their papers as each turned the pages for stories of most interest to them, the front pages caught Wick's eye. He noticed Rose's differed in size from the local paper and had a color photo. He called out the name of the tabloid.

"Mama Watters, what is the *GRIT?*"

She slowly pulled down the paper and smiled. "It's a national weekly, full of good news and positive features. As a matter of fact, this edition is the first time they've run a color picture. See the American flag?" said Rose as she held up the June 1963 issue of the *GRIT.*

Wick wanted to know more about the paper. Where was it headquartered and how did they sell it? Where had she gotten it? Rose explained the paper was published in Williamsport, Pennsylvania, and that her copy was by subscription. She noted they did sell single copies through newsboys who delivered them in small towns all over the country. Then she showed him the inside back cover where a recruiting ad appeared for delivery boys.

Wick's eyes grew bigger and his mouth wider. "Really? I'm going to write them on Monday!"

Details in the ad confirmed one had to be at least thirteen to deliver the paper. The *GRIT* would be drop-shipped to the designated address on Friday afternoons. Copies sold for 15 cents. Wick would keep a dime and send a nickel back to the company for every copy sold. He decided on fifty copies for his first order, Mama Watters reminding him he could increase it at any time.

This was more than throwing papers on lawns and front porches, thought Wick. This was like "special delivery"—hand-to-hand, face-to-face sales and a partnership with a big company, yet he was free to develop his route and clientele. In essence, he would be running his own business and getting to know his customers firsthand. He was anxious to get started.

In just three weeks, he increased his order to one hundred copies. From Fox Manufacturing in north Rome, where Wick would pedal his bike up to the roll-out windows as the ladies in the stitching department came over to buy the latest *GRIT,* to the First National Bank downtown on Second Avenue where president Danforth Jacobs awaited his weekly copy, Wick diligently covered his well-cultivated territory.

He was an ambitious teenage entrepreneur, and he would never forget the experience nor the loyal customers who made it possible.

Chapter Six

When in Rome

Rome, Georgia, founded in 1834, is a city of seven hills (Blossom, Jackson, Lumpkin, Mount Aventine, Myrtle, Neely, and Shorter) and three rivers (Etowah, Oostanaula, and Coosa). As such, it bears semblance to its namesake in Italy. Ancient Rome indeed was built on seven hills, with the Adriatic, Ionian, and Mediterranean seas surrounding it (seas, not rivers, but close enough if one is mythologically minded).

Detailing the flow of the rivers is as meandering as they are: The Etowah originates from the Blue Ridge Mountains in Lumpkin County, flowing southwest to join the Oostanaula, having been formed by the confluence of the Conasauga and Coosawattee in northwest Georgia. The two rivers meet in downtown Rome to form the Coosa, which rambles southwesterly through neighboring Alabama until joining the Tallapoosa River near Montgomery to become the Alabama and then Mobile rivers, which empty into Mobile Bay and the Gulf of Mexico.

Clock Tower (Rome's iconic City Clock Tower and Courthouse Spire)

To anyone who grew up in Rome, why complicate things? To them, it's the Coosa all the way down.

In front of Rome's city hall sits a statue of the iconic Capitoline Wolf with Romulus and Remus, the mythical twins who were rescued by the she-wolf and later fought to the death over naming their new city near the Tiber River, with brother Romulus prevailing. A gift from old Rome, it is an exact replica of the art form situated on the Palazzo dei Conservatori on Campidoglio in Rome.

Most Romans in Georgia were pleased with their gift until Benito Mussolini sided with Adolf Hitler at the onset of World War II. When Italy's pompous, fascist dictator declared war on the Allies in 1940, locals reacted overtly, including threats to dynamite the statue. The city commission had it crated and banished to the city hall basement. Twelve years later, art-minded and history-conscious constituents lobbied the commissioners to reconsider. In 1952, the trio were returned to their pedestal in front of City Hall.

By that same year, Reed Watters was equally pleased. Not only had the statue been rescued from its cellar confinement, but sales of his popular Brunswick stew had experienced an upward trajectory. He became landlord to fourteen residential and two commercial properties downtown. Reed also acquired forty-two acres paralleling the Oostanaula River at the south end of Bells Ferry Road, and built a rustic four-bedroom cabin with a creek stone fireplace and ample screened porch overlooking the "Oost." It hugged the banks of the landmark river and had the feel of a country cottage. More than a cabin, it would become a haven for contentment.

The acreage along the Oostanaula was not unfamiliar territory for Reed. Back in the days when he was courting Rose, her parents owned land farther up the river. Reed's horse "Blaze" knew the mile-long trail between the two farms well. He would hitch the horse to the wagon and proceed to pick up Rose, always on time. Following an evening of picnicking by the river, illuminated by the brilliant moonlight sifting through the Georgia pines, Reed would signal Blaze it was time to return Miss Rose home. After giving Reed a peck on one cheek and once she was safely inside, he would climb back into the wagon with the usual instructions, "Take us home, Blaze."

About one minute into the return trip, Reed would nod off, the reins limp in his hands and Blaze on cruise control.

Many years later after Reed passed away, Rose convinced herself she should renew her drivers' license. She literally had not driven in five years. Reed had always driven them wherever they needed or wanted to go. Uncle Albert drove her to the state patrol licensing facility where she would have to take the written exam and a dreaded, unnerving driving test in his 1956 Packard. Passing both with no hitches, she had Albert take her to the Chevrolet dealer across town, where she bought a brand-new lime green Corvair that same afternoon. Few cars were equipped with factory air-conditioning in those days, so Rose had it installed. The model was one of the first "compacts," so it didn't take long to feel like you were riding in a refrigerator instead of an automobile.

Weeks later, young Wick was seated in the back as Rose gave her cousin Nettie a test ride down a familiar country road under a beaming sun and clear blue sky. Nettie was impressed with all the bells and whistles this small vehicle included. Long before tinted windows became popular, the dealer had added a tinged strip across the top of the windshield.

As Rose talked on about the new minister coming soon to

North Rome Methodist Church, Nettie interrupted, gazing up at the sky through the tinted upper windshield. "Rose, I do declare. I believe it's coming up a cloud."

His grandmother just kept talking and smiling, while Wick restrained himself from laughing out loud.

Chapter Seven

Uncle Tom

Over time, Reed accrued some celebrity because of his popular brand, though certainly not any he sought. The *Rome News-Tribune* had featured a two-page spread when he opened the plant on Reynolds Street in north Rome. A new independent business was always good news for loyal subscribers, and the exposure elevated the owner's profile in the community. So occasionally passersby would say or think, "There goes Uncle Tom," when Reed strolled down Broad Street.

Reed wasn't the namesake of his stew, though. That title was reserved for a special friend of the Watters family.

Thomas Sequoyah Prophett, born in 1889, had grown up with Reed, both swimming all three rivers, as Watters's seven boys would many years later.

Wick's favorite swimming story was of his dad, Raleigh, who as a young boy once swam with a broken arm from a tree climbing adventure. Rose had warned him not to go swimming until the doctor removed the cast, but Raleigh could not resist. Determined to swim in the cool Etowah on that sizzling summer day, he stroked with his right arm while holding the left above the water. Intermittently turning on his back, the daring Watters's plaster cast resembled a crooked telescope on a submarine. Even with confidant Tom imploring him to be careful, Raleigh was determined to swim. Raleigh could always count on his Cherokee friend for sound advice.

Like so many others of their generation, Tom Prophett and Reed Watters would survive the Great Depression by adapting, repairing, and enduring, using the most powerful tool of all—their imaginations. Occasionally able to visit the DeSoto Theatre in downtown Rome, their 15 cents bought more than a movie, popcorn, and soda. It was an escape that allowed them to dream of the day they could cast off the shackles of "doing without" and instead "make do."

For Christmas, Reed would bring home a crate each of apples and oranges, setting one on either side of the fireplace. Santa would bring each son a new set of roller skates. When those skates were worn out, the boys would remove the good wheels and affix them to a scrap board. Decades later, that humble homemade version would evolve into the highly commercialized skateboard, eventually introduced as a sport in the Summer Olympics.

Prophett was a tall, soft-spoken, patient man who viewed common sense as the denominator of life. He was half American Indian, his Anglo father having wed a full-blooded Cherokee from North Carolina. Tom was given the name Sequoyah in honor of the most influential Indian in the Cherokee Nation. In the mid-1800s, Sequoyah invented the syllabary that enabled translation of the Cherokee language into English, thereby educating the tribe to become the most literate among their Indian peers.

At nineteen, Tom married a beautiful and petite young woman of Cherokee descent. Aiyana, meaning "eternal blossom," was indeed his gentle flower. They both wanted children, but only two years into their marriage, Aiyana was diagnosed with leukemia. Tom was crushed, working two jobs to ensure his wife had the best care possible. In those days, medical insurance was scarce and affordable for the elite only.

He was by her side every night as the leukemia continued to ravage Aiyana's blood cells. In just eight months she was gone, and Tom was all alone. She had made him promise he would find another wife to sustain and enrich his life, but it was a promise he simply could not keep. No woman, he well knew, could ever replace Aiyana. Tom would never remarry.

He was proud to be an American while embracing his Cherokee heritage. He was content with life and believed a man's character ultimately defined that life. Prophett considered himself a rich man, believing his values and integrity were his wealth and his two years with Aiyana an eternal blessing.

As they grew into their late twenties, Tom admired Reed's entrepreneurial spirit, his drive to make something, build something, and an innate curiosity to listen and learn. Though Darlington School and the Cotton Block had served him well, Reed's friendship with Tom was a bond of trust and truth, wisdom and wonder that no textbook or merchant could match.

Tom became like family to the Watters, so much so that Reed called him "uncle" from time to time. Prophett brought with him a darned good recipe that Reed, after adding a meat and infusion of secret sauce, turned into the proprietary Brunswick stew.

Tom worked at Pepperell, a textile mill located to the south of Rome in Lindale, for thirty-eight years as maintenance supervisor.

If any equipment broke or shut down, the first call was to Prophett. His job was demanding yet the mission simple: Keep the looms weaving at peak efficiency and the executive office smiling. All that was about to change in the spring of '49.

Prophett had been a regular at the Watters farm on weekends and many an evening fishing in the Oostanaula. Before the processing plant was even a dream, he kept the kettle fire flickering and the stew stirred, whether for a family outing or a batch to cater to the Methodists at Morrison Campground, a Methodist retreat not far away in Kingston, where many attended summertime and fall revivals. Rose's parents owned the campground, and the spiritual campers loved the taste of the delicious Brunswick stew.

Reed recently had sensed Tom was becoming weary of the textile mill. He discussed with his brother Burton and they both agreed that, before plans for a processing plant were underway, Reed would approach Tom about their idea.

On a Saturday night, with the Oost flowing and the frogs croaking in the background, Reed handed Tom a cold Pabst Blue Ribbon as they sat down on the large party deck overlooking the river.

"You're not happy at the cotton mill. Am I right?"

Tom glanced over at Reed and hesitated. "How did you know that?"

"I spent many a day down at the Cotton Block and learned how to read every mind. Whether a man's buying or selling, his face, especially his eyes, say what his mouth won't speak.

"We've been good friends since grade school, Tom. I value our relationship, and Rose and our family appreciate and trust you infinitely. I want to make you an offer."

Tom's eyes opened wider as he took another sip of his beer.

"Burton and I are committed to going forward with plans to construct a canning plant in north Rome. We would like you to live here, manage the farm, and become permanent stew master for all outdoor cooking and catering. In return, we'll build you a two-bedroom cabin on the north end of the river. I'll double what you're making at the mill now. All you need to do is shake my hand. It's better than any contract."

A speechless Prophett, with a detectable tear in the corner of each eye, extended his hand. That night he officially became "Uncle Tom," and when it came time to brand the stew, no other name was even considered. "Uncle Tom's Famous Brunswick Stew" with Prophett's likeness in his signature blue frock coat and wide-brim, open-crown hat would appear on the classic label.

Chapter Eight

Anchored in Alaska

Not long after its opening in 1949, Watters Canning Company's proprietary version of the stew became a regional favorite. "Uncle Tom's Famous Brunswick Stew" became the number-one-selling brand in the Deep South—so good that travelers from other regions of the US would pack cans of the southern delight to take back home, and locals would carry it with them on trips as far away as Alaska and Maine.

Wrote an ardent "Uncle Tom's" fan from afar:

> Elmendorf Air Base
> Anchorage, Alaska
> 19 August 1954

Mr. R. L. Watters
9 Reynolds St.
Rome, Georgia

Dear Mr. Watters:

At last, we have had our feast, the pictures are made and I am enclosing them. Heavy rains and floods have prevailed here for a

Uncle Tom's Famous Brunswick Stew (original label)

month and we have had numerous power failures. These pictures were made by the light of a single bulb as we dared not use the floodlights for fear we would cause the lights to fail. Construction goes on here day, night, rain, and come what may, while the weather is not too cold, and our lines are overloaded. Hardly a day passes that we are either without electricity, hot water, or heat for at least four hours and often it will occur twice a day, still it is not a hardship but an inconvenience. I sincerely hope this situation is different before winter comes or some Georgia people are going to freeze!

The group picture shows all of the guests except one couple who were transferred to Fairbanks the day before the party; however, they did get a taste of the stew for I gave them some. Beginning at the left is Lt. Wade Jernigan of Cartersville; Capt. Marco Alonzo of Santa Fe, New Mexico (he was formerly stationed in the South and learned to love our Brunswick stew); Lt. Barry Harper and Mrs. Harper (on his right) of Cartersville. Mrs. Harper is the former Jennifer Chrysler and her father is one of your customers. He is Alan Chrysler and was formerly in charge of the meat market at Nationwide in Adairsville. I bought my first stew in this store. Mrs. Holly Formby & Lt. Formby of Ball Ground, Georgia; Mrs. Dan Genoa & Capt. Genoa of Chicago (this couple also considered the stew their favorite dish when they were in the South).

To give you some idea of how much we enjoyed the stew, that small group of people consumed two gallons of stew, along with 57 biscuits; a gallon of salad and a whole chocolate cake plus 60 cups of coffee. There were some happy but FULL folks after that feast.

Our Alaskan newspapers are dominated by editorials and opinions on statehood for them but have very little news from the

States. About the only way we know what is going on in Georgia is to read the <u>Bartow Herald</u>, and it is a month old when it arrives. A Seattle newspaper costs 50 cents per copy up here!

Thanks again for your kindness.
Sincerely yours,
Mrs. Wallace A. Jackson
Box 434, A.P.O. 249
c/o Postmaster, Seattle, Washington

Chapter Nine

Bahama Blue

Oostanaula High School was situated near the banks of the river, not far from the Watters farm off Bells Ferry Road. Though one of the smaller schools in Floyd County with a student population of about 640, it was one of the few with all students—first through twelfth—contained on one campus in one building. It would be a couple years after Wick graduated before separate primary and middle schools were built.

It was also uncommon for students to start and finish at the same school. Including Wick, a total of only fifteen graduates in his class of 106 had attended all twelve years together.

"O High," as it was called, enjoyed a good reputation both academically and athletically. At the high school level, its faculty was fortunate to have so many dedicated, well-degreed teachers. The English and math curriculums consistently produced high achievers who scored well on the SATs, the aptitude litmus test required by most universities and colleges.

The football team excelled too. As menacing and evasive as

their chosen mascot, the Oostanaula Otters were all about speed, but size, not so much. Head Coach Stance Stagg took a smaller but quicker team to the finals in 1961 to shut out bigger, perennial favorite Lincolnton 21–0 in capturing O High's first of three state championships. In the late '70s, the *Atlanta Journal-Constitution* listed the Otters among the top ten winningest teams in the state, across all classes. Wearing all-black uniforms with tan stripes down the pants legs, the center of the helmet, and on jersey numbers, the squad appeared deceptively smaller than opposing teams.

Wick needed all the help he could get in 1965 when he told father Raleigh he was going out for football. Weighing in at only 106 pounds, he convinced himself he could make the team, though Wick knew he would have to gain about fifteen pounds between spring training in March and the season opener in late August. He would need to eat like a bear if he was going to be an Otter.

Wheat germ, milk shakes, malts, and yes, bigger helpings of Brunswick stew were regulars on Wick's menu. After six months, all he could add to his small frame was a disappointing six pounds. Yet he made the team, though the game program listed the sophomore halfback at 120. Coach Stagg was employing a little psychology perhaps to boost Wick's confidence and at the same time not advertising O High had a player in the featherweight category.

Thanks to tenacious defense, the Otters had a remarkable season, shutting out their opponents for nine games and three quarters until Gordon Lee managed a fourth quarter field goal. Though Wick rode the bench, Stagg did put him in two games that had become runaways. To "letter," a player had to participate in at least three quarters.

The prospects for that third quarter and a coveted athletic

jacket looked promising as the Otters began spring practice in Wick's junior year. Still, at only 112 pounds, that goal of 120 seemed less likely. A stubbornly high metabolism just wouldn't allow Wick to retain any added weight.

He would remember those people, including his parents, who tried to dissuade him from going out for football. He wasn't big enough, they said, and those players twice his weight would mow him down. It was a legitimate dream, but a dangerous one.

He continued to dismiss them all. He was going to make it through spring practice, make the roster, and at some point in the season earn his letterman's jacket, with or without 120 pounds. Midway through spring practice, Wick had an opportunity to shine.

The offense, like the defense, would split up into groups to focus on one-on-one drills. The idea was mano y mano, for it was more macho. In Wick's case, the second- and third-string running backs would take turns lining up at the receiver position to run a crossing pattern over the middle. On assistant coach Larry Brickstone's whistle, the quarterback would take a mock snap from the center and drop back to throw.

Positioned about seven yards away was linebacker Brad Tomb, a burly bison anxious to stomp his prey. The goal was simple. Could the defenseless receiver make the catch, take a broadside hit, and hold on to the football? About the same odds as a VW beetle taking on a Mack truck.

To Tomb, a 195-pound senior headed to Clemson on an athletic scholarship, Wick was raw meat.

Double-checking his chin strap was snapped, Wick awaited Brickstone's cue. The quarterback dropped back to throw, and Wick watched the ball all the way into his hands, tightly cradling it and instantly feeling Tomb's body drive through his and down into the ground. Wick could have lain there for a few seconds, but his brain wouldn't hear of it. He got to his feet immediately, winked at Tomb, then tossed the ball back to the coach with a wry smile. Wick had just absorbed a blow from a touted linebacker and survived.

But the head-on collision with good friend Dexter Whaley in the next drill was what altered Wick's dream. Dexter was a kind, quiet, easygoing, outstanding student in the classroom, but when his 240 pounds walked on to the practice field, he was all business. Line coach Dick Gallows took a group of beefeaters and some running backs over to his corner of the field. The classic "bull ring" was the next exercise.

Everyone was to run in place in the circle while Gallows pointed to a lineman and a back, then on his whistle, both charged full speed into the other. Wick knew he would lose this battle but did not realize the pain he would feel compared to Tombs's hit. It was like running toward an oncoming locomotive. Whaley literally ran over Wick. Wick's arms immediately slid from Whaley's waist as he fell back limp to the ground. For a few moments he could not move as his eyes indeed saw stars. The next thing he saw was not only Gallows but his teammates all gazing down on him, anxiously wondering if he could move. He did, and with one arm extended down from a concerned Whaley, Wick was pulled up onto his feet. Gallows immediately dismissed the drill.

He was embarrassed, but Wick knew in that moment what he had risked by trying to beat the odds as a stubborn 116-pounder. He would not quit on the battlefield nor be so persuaded, but he would finish spring training and then walk into Coach Stagg's office and announce his decision to forego football. As Wick moved through the locker room toward the head coach's office on that following Monday, Stagg was headed out. He stopped and stared at Wick with those renowned steely blue eyes, waiting to hear what he had to say. Then Wick uttered the dreaded four-letter word he had so agonized to speak, almost apologetically admitting he couldn't gain sufficient weight.

Other than a head nod, Coach Stagg did not acknowledge nor offer any comments on Wick's decision, except "follow me" as the head coach turned and led him back through the locker room and out to a study hall he would inhabit for the time being.

Wick learned later from his father that Coach Stagg had planned to switch him to a defensive back before the next season. One of his assistant coaches was impressed with his good speed and quick, sure hands.

If only the head coach had said that to me.

Wick didn't earn a jacket, but he did earn a measure of respect. At least Uncle Tom was content that he had.

Though leaving the gridiron and landing in study hall was embarrassing to Wick, the circumstance proved to be a blessing for him in the long run.

A young lady seated three rows over and two seats up caught his eye. Pretty and poised, she was not chatting with anyone in front or back of her like most of the students in the unmonitored classroom. She obviously took "study hall" literally, as her left hand turned and stopped at different pages in her book while her right wrote down information in her notebook. Her face and physique were definitely easy on the eyes, but Wick was equally impressed with her demeanor. She exuded a confidence and maturity beyond her apparent years.

Too shy to walk over after the bell to introduce himself, Wick learned later from a classmate seated across from her that the young lady's name was Hollie O'Hara. Because he was working nights and weekends at Rowe's supermarket in north Rome, Wick didn't have much time for dating or a relationship. He would not approach Ms. O'Hara during his junior year, though he always savored seeing her face in the crowded hallway when classes changed. God willing, she would still be available come his senior year.

In September 1967, Wick began his final year at O High. Everything was running smoothly at the farm, thanks to Uncle Tom, who had become Wick's confidant and advocate. Now working at the A&P supermarket after school and Saturdays, he cut his hours in half. He was pumped about introducing himself to Miss O'Hara. He had passed up the prom his junior year but now had a strategy set for the '68 dance.

Those headed off to college the next fall most likely would be taking a typing class, as essays, term papers, and reports at the college level had to be typed. Wick checked with his friend Jeanette who worked in the principal's office and had access to the rolls class by class. She confirmed Hollie O'Hara was assigned to Judy Sacul's two fifteen class. Wick immediately went down and registered.

It was open seating the first day and, fortunately for Wick, only eighteen students were on the final roll. As fate would have it, O'Hara had arrived early and was seated on the left side of the room, about three rows back. Wick walked to the back of the room, then turned left to claim a typewriter located conveniently behind O'Hara and one row to the right. Seated three rows up and one desk to the right was his good friend, Jake Lane. As each day progressed, Wick couldn't help but notice that Jake also had designs on O'Hara.

Bottom line, both Wick and Jake flirted with the young lady so much that Mrs. Sacul had to remind Hollie from time to time to turn around and keep her eyes and hands on the typewriter. With Jake now in the picture, Wick could see he must accelerate his plan, *even if by accident.*

Come the Ides of March, as the ringing bell dismissed class, Wick immediately walked up to tap O'Hara on the shoulder.

"Say, Hollie, could I speak to you for a couple minutes?"

"Sure, Wick. Don't tell me you need tutoring in typing," she said, turning around. He liked that she had a good wit too.

"I've got a new VW Beetle. Well, it's not really new. It's a '66 and Bahama Blue, but it would *look* new if you were riding shotgun."

She blushed a little, then smiled. "I would love to accommodate, Wick. When did you have in mind?" He was already impressed that she didn't ask where the shotgun was located.

"How about this Saturday, say I pick you up at noon and we take a picnic lunch out to the Berry College campus?"

"That sounds wonderful! I'll be ready at twelve o'clock sharp."

Wick showed up on Saturday to the Lake Gardens neighborhood in a hand-washed VW, its Bahama Blue well shined. Hollie's natural beauty was even more evident outside the halls of O High. Dressed in a neatly pressed white blouse and bright yellow slacks, sun shades pushed up on her head, and a charm bracelet on her right wrist, she was ready for a picnic.

Wick had iced tea in tow, country fried chicken, potato salad, and of course a side of Uncle Tom's Famous Brunswick Stew. He added lemon bars for dessert. The sky was blue, and not a single cloud could be found.

They were on the Berry campus in twenty minutes, staking out a spot where tall pines provided shade and one of grandmother Rose's quilts made a comfortable buffer on the grass.

In about three hours, Wick and Hollie knew more about each other and their families than any conversation at school would ever yield. Of particular note was the revelation that the two had literally lived only one block apart when their parents resided on Harvey Street off North Broad—she as an infant and he, a toddler. The other revelation would take place after Hollie took the wheel of Wick's VW.

While riding back from the Old Mill, which at the time featured the world's largest water wheel, Wick turned to Hollie and asked, "Would you like to drive?" He would later confess he had no idea why he asked her, other than, "I just had that impulse. Maybe I was a little nervous and reaching for something to say?"

Hollie hesitated, then answered, "Okay, but you'll have to tell me when to turn."

That would have been the optimal moment to retract his question, but Wick pulled over and the two swapped seats.

Though the Berry campus was listed in the Guinness Book of Records as the world's largest, its roads in that area were narrow and almost unpassable for two automobiles. Nevertheless, Hollie took the wheel and got up to about fifteen miles per hour. As they approached their turn, Wick kept waiting for Hollie to commit, but he waited too late to say, "Turn now!" She suddenly jerked the steering wheel to the left, and the car slid across the road to the right, then veered back to the left into a ditch and embankment.

Both Hollie and Wick were stunned by the impact, but neither were hurt. A gentleman sitting on his front porch in one of the college's faculty residences came running down to inquire if everyone was okay and to see if he could help.

Wick confirmed they were fine and thanked him for the quick response. The front left fender indeed was bent back, but Wick's Bahama Blue was still drivable. Hollie was petrified and embarrassed that she had wrecked Wick's shiny Beetle, but he admitted it was all his fault. He should never have asked her to drive in the first place, especially when he learned in the next moment Hollie didn't even have a learner's permit. She would be turning fifteen the next month.

Wow, she really is younger than I thought. Turned out, Hollie was an advanced student, and her parents had been given an option enabling her to exempt the eighth grade at Lake Gardens Middle School and enter high school at age thirteen. Even if this hadn't been the case, Wick still had made a stupid mistake that could have turned out much worse.

Hollie was worried how she would explain the accident to her father and how she would pay for the damages. She had a part-time job at the Big K and offered to send Wick $25 a month until the repair was paid in full.

That's when Wick realized what a precocious young lady she was. He put his arms around Hollie and gave her a tight, reassuring hug.

"It's all right, Hollie. Trust me, I'll take care of it. You don't owe me anything. I owe *you* an apology."

After taking Hollie home, Wick drove to a friend's house and they used a crowbar to bend the fender farther away from the tire. Then he drove home to let his parents know he'd had an accident. He explained he was going too fast when making a turn and the car had slid into a ditch. No other car was involved and, while understandably a little rattled, Hollie was not injured.

Wick's biggest concern now was, would Hollie accompany him to the senior prom, or had he squandered that opportunity?

Hollie was her usual, pleasant self when they next saw one another in typing class, but Wick was having trouble bringing himself to ask the question that he had longed to ask for nearly a year. It became easier, however, when Jake tipped him off that Hollie had been invited by a senior at Darlington to their prom, coincidentally the same night as O High's. She was wavering, believed Jake, because Hollie hinted she had hoped Wick would have asked her, but assumed he was having second thoughts after she wrecked his car.

"You better make your move before she gets away," Jake whispered to Wick, realizing his friend needed a nudge.

There was no chatting or flirting during this class. Instead, Sacul's end-of-semester exam was everyone's focus. All that could be heard was the cacophony of typewriter keys. At the bell, however, Wick wasted no time in leaving his desk to tap Hollie on the shoulder again.

"How did you do, Hollie? Those fingers looked like they were typing at warp speed."

She turned around, relieved the test was over but even more so that Wick had broken the ice.

"Well, I think. How about you?"

"For sure not as good as you, but I believe I'll make the cut." Wick smiled. "I might not be the fastest or most accurate when it comes to typing, but I know a jewel when I see one. I've had the best seat in the house all year, admiring your poise and posture, which isn't easy sitting behind one of these machines. Your beauty and brain make a great combination. My head and heart do too, and they both are inviting you to the senior prom. It would be my honor, Hollie, if you would accept."

Wick waited all of an agonizing ten seconds before she answered, Hollie seemingly in a trance.

"I was afraid you would never ask. Yes, Wick. I would love to accompany you to the prom."

With that, Hollie rose slowly and gave the young man a long, tight hug around the neck.

The two literally danced the night away at O High, and their bond of platonic love and friendship would continue to grow.

Chapter Ten

Scarlet Letter

It was late fall 1967. The sky was full of blue and the sunshine felt good as Wick drove his VW down the winding road home to the south end of the Oostanaula. Though by now the deciduous trees had shed most of their autumn leaves, he could still enjoy those that remained, falling in rich shades of red, yellow, and gold.

O High had released students at midday for the extended Christmas holiday break, and he was anxious to make it to the 12 Polaris Terrace mailbox.

His father was at work at the paper mill. Raleigh was preparing his department for Georgia Kraft's annual shutdown. But he wasn't anxious about it, as he had engineered it fourteen times at this point in his career.

Wick's mother Edith was also busy at work as the bookkeeper/receptionist for the *Rome News Tribune*. If you wanted to see the publisher, Baird B. Mahoney, you had to go through "Blossom," the nickname her father, Julius Beamish, had bestowed on her as a young girl.

Wick's older sister, Diane, was no doubt on the phone at work, where she had followed in her mother's footsteps straight to Southern Bell after her graduation from O High in 1966.

As he pulled the car up to the mailbox, Wick rolled down his window like he was cranking an antique Graphanola. Just as slowly, he lowered the door on the mailbox, almost afraid to look. Wick extended his hand gingerly into the mailbox as if he might find a snapping turtle inside, then cupped his left hand to ensure the capture of every single piece, junk mail included. He slid the contents to the edge of the opening, then reached over with his right hand to pull the papers through the window, laying the stack on his lap.

Wick meticulously removed each item from the top like it was ticking before laying it on the empty passenger seat. When he got to the fifth one down, his eyes froze. This was the gem he had been hoping for. The envelope spoke to him explicitly. The cellophane address window showed his full name, "Watters, Coleman Brunswick," with "Office of the Registrar and Director of Admissions" printed in the upper left corner. In the opposite corner the postmark was stamped, "Athens, GA, Dec 13 '67."

The graphic that rendered him temporarily paralyzed, however, was bold black type printed over a scarlet red ribbon, slanted left to right and running top to bottom declaring "Official Acceptance, The University of Georgia."

Wick stared at the envelope for a couple minutes, embracing it lest an unexpected gust of wind take it from his hands. His mind was flooded with all the opportunities that lay before him, but for now he would relish the fact that the flagship university of the state of Georgia had said "YES."

After opening the envelope and reading the admissions

protocol, he shifted the car into first gear, drove down the peaceful magnolia-lined drive, marched into the house, and shot straight over to the phone. He had to call his mother, father, and sister to share his good news. After that, he laid down on the sofa to savor the moment.

He wished his grandparents, Papa and Mama Watters, were still alive to hear the news too. Reed had succumbed to emphysema in May of 1963, and Rose had suffered a fatal stroke in the same month but in 1967.

At seventy-eight, Uncle Tom was still stirring, both the famous stew and all around the farm he so loved. Wick wanted to tell him in person.

When he arrived at the farm that evening, Wick spotted Uncle Tom easily, as the setting sun silhouetted his signature hat and frock coat. He was standing over a kettle, stirring the last batch of the day. Only a few coals remained in the dimming fire.

Wick parked the VW beside a huge pin oak at the entrance to Uncle Tom's cabin, hopped out of the car, and headed toward the stew master.

"Uncle Tom, Uncle Tom," yelled Wick, waving his letter and walking faster. Tom was still the face of the brand, though Wick's uncles Burton and William had assumed leadership of the company after Reed and Rose's passing. They well understood the value of Uncle Tom's legend.

"Guess what I got in today's mail?"

Uncle Tom placed his hand-carved paddle in a rack beside the kettle.

"All As on your report card? Your scores on the SAT?"

Wick smiled from ear to ear. "Only one A this semester, and this is far better news than my scores on the SAT." Back in the spring, he had retaken the universal exam at the encouragement of his English teacher, Tara Brevard. It couldn't hurt, she said. Historically, some students had improved their scores by as much as 50 to 100 points.

As Wick drew closer to the man, he belted out, "I've been accepted at UGA!"

Uncle Tom immediately reached out with both arms to give Wick a big hug.

"I knew you would, Wick. It was meant to be!"

The two sat down and chatted for a good while, speculating what classes he might take his first quarter, what would be his major, where the dormitories were located, when his orientation event was scheduled over the summer, and would he be pledging a fraternity? The two covered nearly everything as the Oost and its nighttime melodies played in the background.

Chapter Eleven

Delta Epsilon

Wick and Hollie made the most of their summer days in 1968, especially since he would be heading off to Athens in the fall. The forthcoming freshman attended a three-day orientation in late July, required for all incoming students. It was a good experience for him, an eye-opener filled with pointers from upperclassmen, workshops including Q&A time for curious minds, and extracurricular activities encouraging interaction and teamwork among future classmates. The prospect of being one among a projected eighteen thousand students was both exciting and a little overwhelming for young Wick.

Hollie would begin her senior year at O High feeling a void, the absence of a best friend. She managed to navigate through with extra focus on her classwork, preparation for the SAT exam, and the prospects of joining Wick at UGA in the fall of '69. Of course, she would see him when he returned to Rome on intermittent weekends, and they would write one another or talk on the telephone. She had plenty of girlfriends with which to socialize, and Hollie would enjoy senior year traditions and events. Eventually she would get used to her new normal.

On September 29, 1968, Wick was to report to UGA. Raleigh and Edith drove their son the 150 miles to check in to his dormitory, Reed Hall on north campus. Freshmen were not allowed cars.

The ride was a relatively quiet one, more like solemn for Edith. Wick would be the first Watters to attend college, and his mom could not help weaving the memories of their only son through her mind. Raleigh spoke little, until he surprised Wick with an unexpected option.

"You know, Wick, if you wanted to join one of those fraternities, that might be something you could look into."

Almost speechless, Wick mustered up a, "Yes, I just might look into that." His father's only exposure to a fraternity was when the family viewed *The Adventures of Ozzie & Harriet* on Saturday night TV. Singer Ricky Nelson and older brother David were both fraternity men in the sitcom. Their personas were relatively reserved, respectful, and more mature, not the unfortunate stereotype associated with some Greek brotherhoods.

When Raleigh pulled into a space in the Reed Hall parking lot, Edith elected to sit in the car while her husband accompanied Wick to check himself into the dorm. His room was to the west end of the lobby, then two flights down to the partial subbasement. Unlike the full floors above, this small hallway with only four rooms had no resident assistant, or RA. This would prove to be a plus as the fall quarter progressed. The modest room was most spartan, featuring a bunk bed, two small metal desks, two electrical outlets, a window, and a closet. A common shower and restroom were at the end of the hall. In fact, the short hallway was the main feature. The exit door opened out to Sanford

Stadium to the left, and the Bulldog Grill was up the steps to the right in old Memorial Hall.

Father and son walked back up the parking lot to grab Wick's luggage and get a goodbye hug from mom. Edith obviously had been crying at this milestone moment. Her son squeezed her good, holding his mother for what seemed enough time for a cup of coffee. Edith thought back to that moment in Vick's diner when Raleigh had rescued her from fear and then delivered her joy. Wick found out years later his mother wasn't the only one tearing up on the long ride back to Rome.

Wick walked back to his new home, already missing his family, Hollie, and Uncle Tom. His roommate due to arrive the next afternoon, Wick made his bed and lay listening to the street sounds drifting in the lone window. An exhausting day put him to sleep sooner than he thought. Tomorrow he would wake in Athens, the first day of a new chapter in his young life.

When his roommate, Frank, arrived late the next afternoon, Wick was ready to take in the campus, learning the lay of the land for his first quarter of college. His classes would begin early, but he didn't need an alarm clock. A dumpster was un-strategically positioned in the corridor near their window, and a huge roaring truck with robotic arms grabbed up its prey every weekday at six thirty a.m.

Navigating a hilly campus could be daunting for lowly freshmen. Wick's first class, conditioning exercise, was down the hill just off Lumpkin at Gainey Gym. Unintentionally maybe, it was a good way to start the day to prepare one's body for the daily up-and-down foot crusade across campus. Case in point, he had five minutes to reach his next class, world geography, up nearly one hundred steps beginning underneath the Sanford Stadium bridge.

After a late lunch in Bolton Dining Hall, Wick returned to his room to review reading assignments and prepare for his next class. He then hopped the university bus to the Pharmacy Building for Math 101. He had microeconomics on Tuesday and Thursday nights, six to eight o'clock, in the old Commerce-Journalism building. Problem was, the buses stopped running at five o'clock and Wick's math class ended at five forty-five, giving him only fifteen minutes to make his economics class. It seemed a marathon from South Campus, down the hill, then up to Old College on the north end.

By the time the fall quarter ended, Wick's feet were well acquainted with the landscape. All the effort had been worth it. He was all smiles, as everyone back home would be too, when his posted grades averaged a cumulative 3.6, placing the first-quarter freshman on the coveted dean's list. Wick's confidence and momentum carried him through the winter and spring quarters, yielding As and a few Bs in the core curriculum. Wick Watters had made the dean's list in back-to-back-to-back quarters.

Likewise, a confident Wick returned to the banks of the Oostanaula full of optimism, content with his academic achievement. All the while, Hollie's senior year at O High had been rewarding too. She was named valedictorian of the 1969 class and also had been accepted at UGA. There was plenty to celebrate.

Raleigh and Edith hosted the Watters and O'Hara families, along with many friends at the farm. Included was live music and plenty of good food. And of course the best Brunswick stew around, and the best stew master behind the kettle. Uncle Tom couldn't have been more content.

"You're on the road to a rainbow," Uncle Tom told Wick that evening as the celebration was winding down. "A dean's lister, supported by a proud and loving family. Your biggest admirer, Miss Hollie, adds even more color to that arc. Stay grounded, my young friend. Don't take anything or anyone for granted in your journey."

Wick's sophomore year began with Hollie now the new freshman. Her high school grades and SAT scores were considerably higher than his, and her first-quarter grades would sustain that trend. Her dormitory was situated near the corner of Baxter and Lumpkin streets, and she and Wick would meet for lunch at Bolton Dining Hall daily. That and spending ample amounts of time at the library became routine. Like her senior year at O High, the regimen kept her focused. She thrived with structure.

Wick, not so much.

He was eligible to enter "rush," the voluntary exercise of organized visits to the twenty-six fraternities on campus. The protocol was to visit each for twenty minutes over four nights. After discussing the compatibility and potential of each guest, the membership of each fraternity would then extend invitations to those candidates who garnered a second look. That group was then reduced to those who were deemed worthy of a "bid." Depending on the number of bids a rushee received, each had a choice of which brotherhood he would pledge. Wick wound up with four bids, deciding on Delta Epsilon. He felt comfortable with the brothers he had met and talked with, especially Stan Brumby, a rising senior who took Watters under his wing and, coincidentally, was also from Rome. Brumby had already served in the army, including two years in Vietnam, and would graduate from UGA's law school. He would later serve as the state of Georgia's deputy attorney general.

Hollie was happy for Wick's new affiliation but privately concerned his choice might become a distraction. At the same time, the

Greek system was not appealing to her. While she certainly had the credentials and social skills to join any sorority, Hollie was unsure, uncomfortable in fact, about where she was. She loved Wick, she loved UGA, but the large student population and student/professor ratio became overwhelming, certainly when compared to what she had been accustomed. Soon, the decision would be made for her.

Wick navigated through the pledge period, and he experienced no abuse or hazing up to and including his initiation ceremony into Delta Epsilon. By the end of fall quarter in 1969, Wick Watters was a full-fledged Delta Ep, and Hollie O'Hara had fully decided on her next step.

Sitting together on a bench between classes on north campus, Hollie broke the news.

"Wick, this is not the place for me. I'm so sorry."

"What do you mean? You're killing it in the classroom, and we're here, *together*," a flushed and puzzled Wick said as he leaned in to gaze into her eyes.

"You're content where you are, Wick, and I'm okay with that, but I feel like I can't breathe here. It's intimidating to me. My classes are larger than expected, and it's too crowded for me on campus. I'm not introverted—you know that as well as anyone—but I really haven't been able to get to know any of my classmates. Going to a keg party at the fraternity house doesn't appeal to me."

Wick's stomach was churning.

"Hollie, what are you saying? That you want to leave, go back home? What about us?"

"It's not that I don't love you, Wick, of course I do. We're best friends, but right now, for me, it's best I return home and transfer to Berry College. I've shared my feelings with my parents, and they understand and support me 100 percent.

"We'll have to carry on long distance, like we did last year," suggested Hollie, knowing in her heart that her absence might not necessarily make Wick's heart grow fonder. Only time would tell.

So right there, as the sun shone brilliantly through the colorful collage of autumn leaves adorning the towering trees, Wick and Hollie would embrace. Neither was sure it wasn't the last.

Equally devastated were Raleigh and Edith, but perhaps Uncle Tom the most of all. Had Wick veered off the "road to a rainbow" to which he had referred? Was Wick temporarily distracted in his new world or simply going through a stage in this journey of life?

Evidently both. After Hollie's departure and transfer to Berry, Wick slid into academic mediocrity. No more 4.0s and 3.0s. Instead he got 2.0s and 2.5s, maybe a 3.0 here or there was the new order. The dean's list was no longer a goal or even a consideration. Wick became more friendly and frequent with the girls and a beer than his textbooks and classes. Though Uncle Tom had cautioned him back at the farm not to take anything for granted, he had done exactly that.

His worst lapse led to academic probation after the spring quarter of his junior year. A mandatory summer quarter was critical. He either posted at least a 2.0 or he was out. Neither Wick's parents, nor Uncle Tom, and certainly not Hollie were aware of this ultimatum. When he told each one of them the news, their faces told him how much he had let them down.

He could still hear Uncle Tom's entreaty from years ago, when challenged in life, school, or sports: "If it's to be, it's up to me." Wick repeated those wise words to himself every day and responded with a 2.8 for the summer session.

While he knew it would be easy to blame his fraternity experience for his lackluster grades, Wick knew deep down it was all about his personal commitment to succeed or simply switch to cruise control. As Uncle Tom also told him, "I would rather have an A for effort than a B for just showing up."

The local chapter of Delta Epsilon had about eighty brothers during Wick's time. Like a family, they were all different, with signature personalities from various backgrounds, towns, cities, and states. Three of the young men struck Wick as most remarkable.

Tim Thatcher, the chapter president Wick's sophomore year, was indeed an authentic academic and the recipient of multiple scholarships and grants. He was a model student and role model in leadership for anyone.

Wick remembered the night all the brothers gathered in the house for the broadcast of the first military draft lottery. It was December 1, 1969, and Melvin Laird was secretary of defense for then President Richard Nixon.

Random numbers would be assigned to each birthday. Lower numbers were undesirable, for those recipients would be selected first and most likely sent to Vietnam.

Tim's birthday was matched with the number 4. By contrast, Preston, the best beer chugger in the fraternity and most likely to skip class and land in Las Vegas, drew number 356. It was like a terribly bad dream. Tim was visibly shaken as he walked quietly back to his room.

Good news was to follow, however.

Thatcher qualified for a graduate deferment, having been awarded a full scholarship at the University of Pennsylvania to study for his master's degree in anthropology.

When he heard the news, Wick thought back to the spring when he and Tim sat on the house stairway as the Seeburg Select-O-Matic jukebox blared below them in the vestibule. Since it was an open weekend, the house was virtually empty as the two complemented their cold beers with several replays of "I Got a Line on You" by the group Spirit, among other favorites. Even honor students awarded a full scholarship to an Ivy League school could let their hair down every now and then, thought Wick.

Hans Kensing, from Blacksburg, Virginia, was easy to recognize in any crowd. The barrel-chested junior had recently transferred from the University of Michigan and quickly became a fixture, well liked and respected by all the brothers. He was easygoing and always volunteering to help with any goodwill initiatives adopted by the fraternity.

Physically, Hans was strong as an ox but gentle as a lamb and likewise a gentleman around the ladies. It was customary when any brother had a date or girlfriend over, all brothers were to stand when she walked into the room. Hans was always the first man up.

Fraternities were notorious for hanging nicknames on their brotherhood. Hans was no exception. It was no surprise then when "Bear" was bestowed upon Kensing. He had the broad, furry chest and strong back but the temperament of a teddy.

A sampling of nicknames that stuck with other brothers included, in no particular order: Blue, Bogey Fatty, Fatty Grub, Bunz, Tri-H, Iceman, Seabiscuit, Hunky, Doctor Proctor, Squeezie, Yankee Boy, Piper, Hubie, Esquire, Eskimo, Diamond Jim, Firefly, Moon Pie, Elbow, Crisco, Otter, Spooky, Doorknob, and Senator Ole Buddy.

After Hans's graduation, he was hired by the university as a career counselor for those students who needed some direction on their career path and in knowing what their options might be relative to their degree. He always had time for anyone and stayed in touch with students after graduation to monitor their progress.

Hans also stayed involved with the fraternity as president of the voluntary alumni board. His footprint only grew as he advised the chapter leadership on everything from finances to upkeep of the house. He personally mowed the lawn of the huge antebellum home—a task he enjoyed because it meant he would have regular in-person contact with the brotherhood.

Perhaps Hans's most significant contribution to the fraternity was emphasizing the importance of the brothers' involvement in the community and beyond. He helped change the culture of the membership and profile of recruits. More and more young men became leaders on campus, whether in student government or in charity-based or other philanthropic initiatives.

Three brothers, one a Rhodes and another a Truman Scholar award winner, would volunteer for the military after the September 11, 2001, terrorist attack. Two served in Afghanistan and the other in Iraq. Two of these brothers made the ultimate sacrifice. Hans made sure all Delta Eps remembered their fallen brothers in a permanent way by helping design and build two separate memorials on the east side grounds of the house.

Hans himself would be memorialized eight years later. It had been a goal of his to keep the chapter's finances on track to retire the house mortgage. They did, but Hans did not live to see it. Ironically, on September 11, 2009, Hans Kensing succumbed to cancer. Hundreds of current brothers, alumni, faculty, and friends paid tribute in a special service at the University Chapel on the north campus. Brothers and alumni gathered later on the front lawn of Delta Epsilon to dedicate the "Hans House," affixing a bronze plaque bearing his likeness beside the front door.

Jack Valet was from Conyers, about an hour from Athens. Wick wound up rooming with him, Dave McIntire, and Roy

Sanford. One characteristic of Jack's that was evident early on was his preparation for anything and everything.

Both Valet and Wick were journalism majors, Jack as a pathway to law school, Wick as a newspaper writer. Jack was involved in other endeavors too, not the least of which was the Demosthenian Literary Society. Founded in 1803 and among the oldest in the world, DLS was the quintessential platform for extemporaneous debate. Word around campus was that Jack Valet was among the best.

So, it was no coincidence that on school nights, somewhere between eleven p.m. and one a.m., Jack was seated at a long study table in the middle of the room while his roommates slept soundly in their bunks on either side. He wrote and wrote into the night with the small green shade desk lamp trained on his paper, all the while puffing on a bowl of cavendish in his briarwood pipe. Occasionally, Wick would squint with one eye to see if Jack was still at it. If Uncle Tom could see this, he thought, Tom would give Valet an A for both effort and preparation.

Valet's efforts paid off, big time. After law school, Jack would go on to litigate and win numerous high-profile cases, procuring substantial rewards for his clients. Many of these were historically record sums. He thrived on the pursuit of justice, both for his client and his own ethos. Valet was asked in an interview years later, to what did he attribute his repeated success in the courtroom, when most attorneys would rather settle out of court than go to trial? He answered that he relished going to court. He knew he and his team would always be better prepared. Just like he knew this all those nights between eleven p.m. and one a.m. back at the Delta Epsilon house.

A diving accident off a twenty-foot cliff at Mystic Falls when in high school had done severe damage to his right hip and leg. Doctors were challenged in restoring the acetabulofemoral joint to nearly full capacity. At age seventeen, he walked with a decided limp and the help of a cane. Navigating the walkways and stairways on the hilly Athens campus to get to class wasn't easy, but he never complained of the pain that would manifest itself after a long day. His cane became a fixture, part of him and his identity. The medical technology and surgical techniques available years later enabled the lawyer, whose savvy in the courtroom restored the lives of countless victims and their families by exposing negligence and avoidable accidents, to have his own health restored, eventually rendering his signature cane obsolete.

Jack Valet would continue to excel inside the courtroom and out, generously giving back to his alma mater, fraternity, and favorite charities.

Chapter Twelve

Redemption

It was time to get busy, and he was running out of time.

Wick was facing his final year of college, he hoped. Behind schedule, he would need a total of sixty-one hours of courses to graduate on time with his class of 1972. A normal load was fifteen hours per quarter, or the equivalent of three five-hour courses.

Taking one additional course in the fall, winter, and spring quarters would give Wick an additional fifteen hours, but he would still need one more hour to reach the magic sixty-one. In essence, he would be cramming four quarters into three. His goal wasn't impossible, but Wick's friends and brothers mostly laughed when he volunteered his plan.

That hurt, but not as much as it would for his father, mother, and Uncle Tom, not to mention Hollie, who was ahead of schedule at Berry in Rome and would likely finish by the winter quarter of '73. They had stayed in touch all along, though she had been out on a couple dates to break away from the intensity of her studies and to bridge the loneliness she felt. Wick still had strong feelings for her, and he believed she did for him as well, but the reality was if he failed to graduate, let alone on time, his chances with Hollie might be zero. And could he blame her?

Uncle Tom had written a letter of encouragement to Wick, reminding him of the hard work he had put in at O High and his freshman year at UGA. There was no reason he couldn't replicate and commit to that same effort now. Wick reread the letter on this unusually brisk September Saturday morning as he stood out on the deck. A cool breeze off the Oostanaula chilled his hands, but his heart warmed as he finished the letter.

Uncle Tom had ended with a quote from automotive icon Henry Ford: "Whether you think you can or think you can't, you're right."

Wick was energized, ready to crank his Bahama Blue and head to Athens where he would test his resolve to graduate on time.

By the time he arrived, he had spent two and a half hours of drive time thinking through his strategy and specific courses he would add to each quarter to meet the prescribed twenty. He would consider where the lone, last hour would come from later.

With dedicated, methodical class work and study time, he checked off the fall and winter quarters, their combined forty hours yielding a 2.8 GPA. Now twenty-one to go, he registered for two journalism courses in his major, and two sociology courses for his minor. There were few options for a single hour, but Wick smiled when he discovered the university chorus offered one hour a week in rehearsal for a spring quarter–ending concert in the historic University Chapel.

Wick had sung a few times in the Beech Creek Methodist choir in Rome, but only as a fill-in when they were short a member. Now he would find out if he could sing his way to a diploma.

Every week when he entered the crowded chorale chamber, surrounded mostly by music majors, Wick walked efficiently and silently to the baritone section. Occasionally, when rehearsing the Italian cantata selected for the spring finale, conductor Max Williams would single out a section to sing their part. It might be the altos, sopranos, baritones, basses, or tenors. Whenever he did, Wick nearly broke out in a cold sweat, fearing the conductor would castigate him upon discovering there was an impostor within the baritones. He was capable of covering his voice as he blended with his fellow baritones, but an impromptu soloist Wick wasn't.

Such drama never occurred that quarter, however, and Wick successfully winged his way through the performance in May. The chorus received a standing ovation, and Wick Watters earned an hour's worth of validation.

Another celebration took place on the banks of the Oostanaula that June, albeit smaller. Wick had defied the odds and graduated with his class of 1972. He was happy to be back home with his family and friends, enjoyed sharing thoughts and ideas with Uncle Tom, and especially happy that Hollie O'Hara was there too. They discussed Wick's employment possibilities and Hollie's senior year at Berry. Whatever the time and distance between them, the two would become even closer over the next year.

Colonel Crowley, retired Air Force Reserve and placement counselor/advisor for the "J" school, had met with Wick just before graduation and indicated he might know of a couple opportunities coming up over the next week or two. Despite Wick's mediocre GPA, the colonel was impressed with Wick's senior year "gut check" and recommended Wick to a few of his newspaper contacts in the south.

Chapter Thirteen

Greenville

The Bahama Blue made its way down I-85 toward the capital of Alabama. Wick had received a call from Walt Thompson, managing editor of the *Montgomery Advertiser,* that Colonel Crowley had recommended him for an interview. The daily was one of several newspapers owned by Multimedia, Inc. When he arrived at the downtown address, Wick parked in the side lot, buttoned his shirt collar, and knotted up his necktie, then entered the building lobby around front. He walked slowly but confidently toward the receptionist who flashed a welcoming smile.

"May I help you, sir?"

"Yes, ma'am. I'm Wick Watters. I have a ten thirty with Mr. Thompson," he said, standing as tall as his legs would allow but not leaning against nor on the mahogany counter.

The receptionist called up to Thompson's secretary to announce, "Mr. Watters." Then she explained, "Mr. Thompson's running a few minutes behind schedule but will be down soon to get you."

Wick took a seat, a little anxious as he glanced around the lobby of what appeared to be a 1940s-era building with a floor of large square, alternating black-and–charcoal gray marble tiles and eggshell-colored plaster walls.

"To get you." Were her words prophetic, thought Wick? Would Thompson "get" the best of young Watters in the interview, or was this the classic double entendre? Would this be the home of his first job, or not? Before his mind could mull over the questions, Mr. Thompson descended the stairs to greet the interviewee.

"Hello, Wick. Walter Thompson. Welcome to Montgomery," he said, extending his right hand, to which Wick coupled an equally firm grip.

"Thank you, sir. I appreciate your granting me an interview. Colonel Crowley sends his regards. He spoke highly of you."

Thompson smiled, thanked Wick for the compliment, then led him up the stairs to his office. After the perfunctory icebreakers and questions about Wick's background, the managing editor led him on a brief tour of the offices and newsroom. Though he did not know him personally, Wick recognized Tom Crawford on the copy desk. Crawford had been editor of the *Red & Black,* UGA's school newspaper, would later work in President Jimmy Carter's press office after stints at the *Advertiser* and the *Atlanta Journal Constitution,* and eventually become known as "the dean" of state capitol journalists covering Georgia politics under the signature gold dome.

The two exchanged hellos, and then Thompson led Wick into an anteroom where he was seated at a table with a standard aptitude test in front of him. Thompson set a timer and left Wick alone to navigate the mental exercise. Wick was taken aback. This test had nothing to do with his writing ability but obviously had been given for a reason. Never mind, he would jump through the hoop. Thompson would share with Wick afterward, almost apologetically, that state employment regulations required the test be given to every new employee. Wick smiled and laughed inwardly. He didn't realize he had been hired.

The position was on the copy desk, where he would edit news and write headlines alongside Crawford and two other copy editors. Thompson wanted Wick to begin the following Monday.

The *Advertiser* put him up at the Ramada overnight, which faced toward the stark white Capitol up the hill. The next morning Wick noticed the cloudless sky as he left with his coffee.

He wasn't sure this was the job he wanted, but he had accepted and, like Uncle Tom, would honor his commitment. He had less than a week to find an apartment or rental. The three-and-a-half-hour drive back to Rome would seem even longer.

Back home that Tuesday evening, Wick gave the good news to Raleigh and Edith and was headed out the door to ride over to the farm to share with Uncle Tom as the phone rang. His mom answered the call, then yelled out to Wick that a Mr. Faulkner with the *Greenville News* was calling for him.

Immediately Wick did an about-face and hurried back in the door. Edith smiled at him as she handed over the phone, crossing her fingers with her empty hand.

"Hello, this is Wick."

"Hello, Wick, this is Stan Faulkner, sports editor at the *Greenville News*. My good friend Colonel Crowley, whom I know through the Air Force Reserve, gave me a call last night, said you might be a candidate for a position we have open on our staff. Would you be interested in coming over to Greenville and let's talk about it?"

Wick had to quickly swallow the lump in his throat before answering. "I sure would, Mr. Faulkner, but first I must tell you I just got back from Montgomery this evening. Yesterday, I accepted a job at the *Advertiser* on the news desk. I sure wish we could have gotten together first."

"Oh, I see. When are you supposed to start?"

"Next Monday, sir."

"I understand," paused Faulkner, "but I tell you what. If you can drive over to Greenville tomorrow, you might have a choice to make before next Monday. How 'bout you be here at eleven. We'll talk, then I'll take you to lunch. How does that sound?"

Wick swallowed the second lump. "That sounds great, Mr. Faulkner. I look forward to meeting you."

"Great, Wick. We're on Main Street, right across from the old courthouse. Check in with the receptionist and she'll send you up to the third floor."

"Yes, sir. I'll see you then."

Wick was wide-eyed and flush-faced. When he told his parents the details, they were too.

Then he was out the door again.

"Where you going?" said Edith.

"To see Uncle Tom. I want to tell him in person now before I get on the road in the morning."

When he arrived at Uncle Tom's cabin on the river, Tom was already coming out the door as he heard Wick's Beetle brake to a stop at the split-rail fence.

Tom gave Wick a big hug and of course wanted to know how things had gone down in Montgomery.

"I got the job. Supposed to start next Monday . . . BUT, I just had a call from the sports editor at the *Greenville News* in South

Carolina, and he wants me to drive over in the morning before I go back to Montgomery. It's unreal, Uncle Tom. I spent most of my drive back rationalizing the job on the news desk as a good start and stepping-stone for a staff writer position. However, if the interview goes well tomorrow, I could begin as a staff writer in sports, which could be an even better opportunity and fit for me.

"What would you do, Uncle Tom?"

Tom hesitated, stroking his closely cropped beard as he pondered what might be best for Wick.

He was a man of few but profound words.

"We may never pass this way again, Wick."

Young Watters knew that was Uncle Tom's way of saying yes, don't let this opportunity get away. Point your car toward Greenville.

Wick headed out at six thirty the next morning with the popular Seals & Crofts ballad playing in his mind, thankful that Uncle Tom was content with his decision.

He drove into the parking garage with time to spare. The *Greenville News* building, at the south end of Main Street, was a contrast to the considerably older one he had visited in Montgomery. The horizontal concrete structure was full of parallel rectangular-shaped windows that were recessed to shade some of the afternoon sun. The architectural design allowed the building to glow at night as the newsroom and other departments were busy preparing the morning paper. The *Piedmont,* located on the second floor, was the afternoon paper.

Wick walked down a couple flights of stairs to the street level. Greenville's antique red brick city hall, with the stereotypical bell tower, stood directly across the street from the modern newspaper offices. A huge crane with the classic wrecking ball was staged next to the building, readied for demolition. The new city hall, a tall, shiny, bronze-colored steel-and-glass high-rise just two doors down, was already in service. Wick learned later that the old red brick building didn't give in so easy. The wrecking ball simple bounced back after repeated swings at the antiquated but stubborn edifice. The demolition company finally had to resort to implosion to bring down the mass of bricks.

Wick made his way up the ascending sidewalk and steps into the newspaper lobby. After signing in and clipping on a name tag, he was directed to the elevator around the corner, where he would ride up to the third floor and exit to the left, then take a left again to walk all the way back to the front corner of the building. He passed a few offices on the right wall until the hallway opened up into a large room full of desks and typewriters. Stan Faulkner was typing away behind his.

"Hello, Wick. Come on over and have a seat," said the sports editor who looked to be in his midforties, about the same age as Wick's father.

"Is this your first trip to downtown Greenville?"

"It is, and I'm already impressed," said Wick with a flattering, confident tone.

"That's good to hear, and I think you'll be even more impressed when I tell you what we've been up to around here."

With that, the interview began.

The *News,* with a daily circulation of about 95,000 and Sunday around 105,000, was the largest of the three papers covering upstate South Carolina. The *Spartanburg Herald* and the *Anderson Independent* were good competitors. Faulkner gave Wick an overview of these and other details, then specifics about the opening for a sixth staff writer. High school and college sports were covered thoroughly, which for the latter included Clemson, South Carolina, Furman, Wofford, Newberry, Presbyterian, Catawba, Elon, Davidson, and Gardner-Webb among others.

An added feature to this staff position was exposure to the National Football League. The Atlanta Falcons' training camp was hosted at Furman, and a writer was dispatched daily to file a story on team and/or individual player progress, including any "grim reaper" news, specifically those players who had been cut from the team that particular day. Most Falcons home games in Atlanta were covered by Faulkner or a designated staffer. The opportunities for experience and growth were obvious for Watters . . . *if* he could convince Faulkner he was the man for the job. Colonel Crowley's recommendation carried weight, especially since he and Faulkner remained active in the Air Force Reserve, but an honest assessment of Wick's mediocre academic performance carried negative weight as well.

After emphasizing and explaining his senior year accomplishments to the veteran sports editor, and sharing a few examples of his writing from assignments at the *Athens Banner Herald* in conjunction with his Grady College of Journalism at UGA courses, Wick awaited a response from the man who could alter his course in life.

With eyes peering above oversight readers, Faulkner leaned forward in his swivel chair and extended his hand.

"I'm thinking you need to make a phone call to the *Montgomery Advertiser* to let Walt Thompson know you've received a better offer from the *Greenville News*. Be sure to express your gratitude for his offer and regrets that you had to reverse field, but this is a better fit for you."

Wick's adrenal gland was working overtime now. He had

secured the job. The overload of courses his senior year and commitment to graduate on time had paid off, and Faulkner sensed a fire in Wick's belly that he liked. Ironically, the *Advertiser* was also a property of Multimedia, which gave Wick some relief that he hadn't betrayed the process by reneging on a competitive publication. Things remained all in the family.

Wick would begin work on Monday, June 19, so he had four days to return to Rome, pack, and get back to Greenville on Friday. The company put him up over the weekend at the old Poinsettia Hotel downtown, giving Wick a couple days to locate an apartment. He wound up renting a room at the YMCA for a week, allowing him more time to search and learn the lay of the land.

He would never forget waking up to his radio alarm clock that first Monday morning at the "Y." The newscaster was describing a burglary that had occurred that Saturday night, June 17, at the Watergate Office Building. Five men, discovered by a twenty-four-year-old security guard, were taken into custody for breaking and entering the Democratic National Committee headquarters. Newspapers, including the *Greenville News,* gave the story little play, positioning it on inside pages with an unprovocative headline.

The headlines grew larger, however, as further investigation revealed the burglars were attempting to bug the DNC in the midst of the 1972 presidential campaign.

But bylines, not headlines, were on Wick's mind his first day in the sports department. A "day" was more so an evening. To get out the morning paper, staff began work at three p.m. and released the last pages for the press at eleven that night.

Hank Bremen, assistant sports editor who later in his career would become founding sports editor of *USA Today,* creating a sports section layout with enhanced, relevant stats, was editing copy when Wick's first story landed on his desk. A sidebar on UGA's homophones, Robert Honeycutt, running back from Greenville, and Lynn Hunnicutt, wide receiver/tight end from Rome, explored how two athletes on the same team with names pronounced exactly the same but spelled so differently were alike, or not, off the field.

For Wick's first byline, Bremen inadvertently typed "by Coleman Watters." When the first copies rolled off the press, Hank grabbed a warm copy and brought it back to Wick. Wick smiled and thanked Hank for the personal delivery, waiting until later that evening to remind him he preferred "Wick." It stuck, just like back in 1950 when Aunt Katie anointed him.

The following week, Wick filed a story that ran information a reader later questioned in a letter to the editor. Rupe Armenian, managing editor, called Wick into his office. He was a small, thin man with a full head of gray hair. He would come out of his office with a fresh copy of the day's paper, find an empty desk on which to lay it open, then turn through page by page, scrutinizing each headline, lead, and select body copy while drawing on his cigarette.

"Yes, sir," said Wick, entering.

"I received a letter from a lady who took issue with the information you included in the bio on Coach Dayton at Wade Hampton, and it appears she's right," he confirmed, handing the letter over his desk to Wick.

After reading, Wick told Armenian, "I just assumed—"

"STOP, stop right there," said Rupe with laser eyes focused on Wick and his index finger pointing to a frame on the wall that read: *Never Assume. It makes an ASS out of U and Me.*

"I'm very sorry, Mr. Armenian. It won't happen again," said Wick, handing him back the letter.

"We all make mistakes, Wick. That's why we proof the paper, but never let it be because we assumed anything. And call me Rupe." He smiled.

Wick never assumed anything in print again.

After the morning paper went to press that night, Rupe, Hank, and fellow writers Bobby Thorne, Gerald Getty, David Powell, and Rudy Smith walked over to Baka's tavern in the next block for a couple pitchers of beer. Baka enjoyed the *News* crew. The affable Greek stayed open till midnight and would play an old 78 rpm vinyl on the turntable behind the bar as he came around to dance like Zorba for the thirsty newspapermen.

Chapter Fourteen

Legends

Over the next two years, Wick would have the opportunity to meet and interview some legends in the sports world.

His first commercial flight on an Eastern Airlines "Whisperjet" in February 1973 was to cover a basketball double header in old Chicago Stadium. The press box was uniquely located at the long end of the court. Loyola vs. Marquette was first up, then Illinois against South Carolina, coached by Frank McGuire. Riding over on the team bus with the gentleman coach was special, but hailing a cab back to the hotel downtown was not. The lady inside the arena office, who called one for Wick, added a warning: "When you hear the car horn blow, run out the door and don't stop running until you're inside the cab." The aging stadium was not located in the best of neighborhoods.

Walking up from "Mother's" basement nightclub to Rush Street with a fellow writer from the *Columbia State Record* presented a challenge. Known for its bitterly cold, brutal winds,

Chicago's "Hawk" forced the two sportswriters to cling to a light pole, without which they would have tumbled down to Division Street.

Wick had the opportunity to meet several legends at the annual Shriners Celebrity Golf Tournament for charity in Spartanburg, South Carolina.

He had just finished his round after arriving late. A caddy drove the cart into the club garage as one of the greatest of all time stepped out and was handed a cold can of beer that he popped open immediately. Wick took a chance and followed the cart inside.

"You look like you could still hit one over the center field wall, Mick," said an admiring but tentative Wick. "Got time for a quick question or two?"

"Do you mind?" the golfer shot back, obviously perturbed and sweating profusely. "I just got off the course and would appreciate a little privacy."

Mickey Mantle had turned him down, but that was okay by Wick. After all, he had invaded the man's space, but he would rather have been scolded by a living legend than have regrets over a missed opportunity.

Bobby Richardson, also a former New York Yankee and at the time the head baseball coach at South Carolina, was there too. While Billy Martin was Mantle's best friend in his playing days, Mantle would grow closer to Richardson as the two grew older. Twenty-two years later, Richardson's abiding faith and friendship would inspire Mantle to redemption before the baseball legend passed at Baylor University Medical Center. The liver transplant he received had come too late, as the cancer had already spread to his lungs.

Doug Sanders was also on display, literally. Few pro golfers ever outdressed the native of Cedartown, Georgia. His personality was just as colorful as his attire and made him a fan favorite, especially at celebrity events. His wide-legged, short swing suited his game, and he won twenty PGA tournaments over his career.

"Country" Don Maynard seemed to feel at home at the Spartanburg tournament. The Pro Football Hall of Famer (1987) was Joe Namath's favorite receiver with the New York Jets. Wick noticed the quick, sure-handed receiver seemed as at ease with a straw hat and club as he did with a helmet and cleats.

Wick encountered other memorable and intriguing legends along the way while working for the *Greenville News*.

Greenwood, fifty-four miles south of Greenville, was the destination for Wick's interview one day. Hoyt Wilhelm and Wick sat down in the empty dugout of Legion Stadium, home of the Atlanta Braves single-A minor league club. One of the best knuckleballers of all time (only Phil Niekro had better stats), the native North Carolinian pitched for nine MLB teams over his twenty-year career and was the first relief pitcher inducted into the Hall of Fame (1985). Amazingly, he didn't make it to the big leagues until he was twenty-nine but made the most of his knuckler, pitching until he was fifty. He retired from the game in 1972, and the Atlanta Braves immediately hired him to manage Greenwood in 1973. Wick was in the right place at the right time to interview another legend.

On a separate trip to Chicago, Wick had an invitation to attend a reception at the Drake Hotel. The room on this occasion was small and crowded, but Wick's eyes grew bigger when he noticed the older gentleman seated near the window in the darkened room. Wick had planned to give the reception a perfunctory nod, but had everyone else not been standing, he might have missed this iconic moment. There sat John Wooden, the greatest college basketball coach of all time.

Wick walked over to introduce himself, standing while a visibly tired Wooden remained seated. Beyond the ten NCAA championships (including a record seven straight) to which he led UCLA over his twenty-seven-year career, the man was a mastermind in leadership and philosophy. Hence the nickname "Wizard of Westwood."

"It is indeed a pleasure and privilege to meet you, Coach Wooden," said Wick in a massive understatement. Basketball was the last thing on Wick's mind at that moment. He was most interested in the man, and Wick quickly led the conversation in that direction. Near the end of their discussion, Wick cited his two favorite quotes of Wooden's: "If you don't have time to do it right, when will you have time to do it over?" and "Success is peace of mind, which is a direct result of self-satisfaction in knowing you did your best to become the best you are capable of becoming."

John Wooden would live to be four months shy of one hundred years old, and he had shared a precious twenty minutes of it with Wick.

South Carolina had been hungry for a winner and a football championship for some time. Paul Dietzel was hired in 1966 to lead them to one. His credentials included a national championship. Having coached under Bear Bryant at Kentucky, the Ohio native became head coach at LSU in 1955 at only age twenty-nine and led the Bayou Bengals to their first national title in 1958 with the famous "Chinese bandits" defense. He left in 1962 for West Point to coach Army, becoming the first nongraduate to do so. Restoring them to their heyday proved to be an uphill battle, especially during the unpopular Vietnam War years. USC offered Dietzel a lucrative, long-term contract, and he mustered an ACC championship in 1969, but recruiting against SEC teams proved a challenge.

Wick spoke with the affable coach down on the field during pregame warm-ups before the Gamecocks' contest against archrival Clemson.

Dietzel treated Wick more like a friend than a sportswriter. Bear Bryant allegedly had told him once he was "too soft" to be a head coach. LSU dispelled that assertion. Wick came away from his conversation believing the opposite, that Dietzel's engaging personality was exactly what connected him with his players and coaches and any success he might have. Wick was reminded of the legendary Georgia Tech coach Bobby Dodd, who believed in consistently praising his athletes. To borrow a quote from John Wooden, "Do not let what you cannot do interfere with what you can do."

Paul Dietzel was an innovator and communicator, a marketer and proponent of praise. The relationships he maintained and sustained with his players long after the gridiron confirmed that.

Annually, in the run-up to the fall football season, the *Greenville News* sponsored a fish fry at a rustic camp near town, hosting coaches and their staffs, along with other sportswriters in the Palmetto State. Frank Howard had retired after thirty years as Clemson head coach, though he remained on the payroll as athletic director until 1974.

Howard was the guest speaker in 1973, and it was always a treat *anytime* the coach spoke, on or off the record. Sometimes the language could be a little salty, crusty, or plain off-color. A guard in his playing days at Alabama, Howard did not like facial hair on his athletes. Mustaches, no. Beards, don't even think about it. Everyone belly laughed when the coach shared his thoughts on the subject, but Wick and every other sportswriter present knew he couldn't print it. Still, Howard was the quintessential icebreaker, and this was a locker-room audience. Women had not yet joined the sportswriting world.

Two quotes that were printable from the beloved coach included, "The score is tied, and we're winning" and "I finally retired for health reasons. The alumni were sick of me."

In the end, Howard let his record on the field do the talking, winning more games—165—than any Clemson coach to that point.

Jerry Stovall was also present that evening. A former unanimous All-American halfback at LSU (1962), selected to the College Football Hall of Fame (2010) and a first-round pick of the St. Louis Cardinals (1963) in the NFL, he was now on the coaching staff for Paul Dietzel at South Carolina. That relationship would benefit him down the road.

Stovall had been a favorite of Wick's growing up, finishing runner-up to quarterback Terry Baker of Oregon State for the Heisman Trophy. When Wick walked down the line getting IDs for a group photo the *Greenville News* photographer had just taken, he looked up at the six-foot-two-inch figure, now wearing glasses. He seemed a little familiar, but Wick wasn't sure who the man was.

"Jerry Stovall," he volunteered as Wick readied to write in his reporter's notebook.

"Jerry Stovall? THE Jerry Stovall?" Wick repeated.

The coach smiled and graciously confirmed it was in fact him, while Wick, now twenty-two, felt like he was twelve all over again.

The man was special for a number of reasons. Beyond his stats, big plays, and awards, no one could have known at the time this would be the person to replace Bo Rein after his tragic death in January 1980.

By that time, Dietzel had departed South Carolina to return to LSU as athletic director. Seventeen-year head coach Charles "Cholly Mac" McClendon had been eased out. Rein, thirty-four, had won two ACC titles at NC State where he had previously coached under Lou Holtz. Holtz coincidentally had already turned down the LSU job but in turn recommended Rein to Dietzel. Bobby Bowden at Florida State and George Welsh at Virginia had also previously declined.

Rein was hired and on January 10 boarded a chartered flight to Shreveport for recruiting. Somehow the plane lost radio contact and drifted off course, crashing into the Atlantic Ocean.

All of a sudden, a job for which he had not been considered became Stovall's.

The humbled and gracious new coach told the LSU Board of Supervisors, "I would give up any job, I would give up my right arm if it meant Bo Rein could come back. I love LSU, but the loss of Coach Rein makes the conditions sorrowful."

Stovall would coach LSU for four seasons, in 1982 finishing eleventh in the AP poll with an Orange Bowl berth against #3 Nebraska. He was named National Coach of the Year by the Walter Camp Foundation and SEC Coach of the Year.

For Wick, Stovall's values, humanity, and commitment to his alma mater made him Man of the Year that evening.

"The Dutchman," he was called by many; then there were some who called him something else.

Wick anxiously awaited his first visit to the Falcons camp at Furman University. He was ten years old when he and father Raleigh watched the 1960 NFL Championship game between the Philadelphia Eagles and Green Bay Packers. The television may have been black and white, but Norm Van Brocklin played like living color. He and his dad enjoyed pulling for the underdog in most games, and it certainly applied here. The Eagles hadn't won a championship since 1948. Van Brocklin, who had quarterbacked the Los Angeles Rams to the 1951 NFL title, had been traded to Philadelphia—some said because his best days were behind him, while others believed his difficulties were due to his conflicts with Rams management.

Van Brocklin's strong, accurate arm led the Eagles to victory. He was named the league's MVP and would be inducted into the NFL Hall of Fame in 1971, the year before Wick would meet the Dutchman.

His legendary temper was a double-edged sword. His intensity and fiery temper fueled his will to win on the gridiron but also got him in trouble off the field. As a coach, his disposition with the press and management cast him in a bad light. Not so with his players. They may have thought he was an SOB, but at the end of the game or their careers, they knew he had made them better players.

Much like General George S. Patton, Van Brocklin was stubborn, demanding, and a disciplinarian. Neither man tolerated sloth, weakness, or insubordinates.

Nevertheless, Wick was anxious to see which Van Brocklin he would find. Wilt Downing, sports information director for the Falcons, greeted Watters and led him over to where the coach was talking to a couple guests. When they finished, Wilt stepped in.

"Coach, I would like you to meet Wick Watters, new writer with the *Greenville News*."

Van Brocklin flashed a smile with a squint, as the afternoon sun was beaming down directly overhead. Then he reached out with the large hand that had passed for 23,611 yards.

"Hello, Wick. Nice to meet you. Did you grow up around here?"

"No sir. I grew up in Rome, Georgia. My dad and I watched you win the championship in 1960. It's an honor to finally meet you. I admire your career and success."

With that, the only thing that had been broken was the ice. A pleasant and cordial Van Brocklin thanked Wick with another smile and turned to walk down to the practice field. The next time Wick interacted with the coach was in Atlanta–Fulton County Stadium. Bremen had assigned him to cover the Falcons against the New Orleans Saints. After the game, he left the press box to ride the elevator down where he joined other sportswriters in the interview alcove.

The Falcons had won, so Van Brocklin was relatively relaxed, though he did seem irritated with a couple of the writers' questions. It wouldn't have been normal had he not. He sipped from a cup throughout the press briefing, and Wick wondered if the contents might have included some kind of elixir?

Doctors had recently removed a benign tumor from Van Brocklin's brain. One needling writer asked Van Brocklin exactly what kind of surgery he'd had.

"It was a brain transplant. They gave me a sportswriter's brain to make sure I got one that hadn't been used."

Chapter Fifteen

Fort Knox

One year near Thanksgiving, Wick could see something hanging from the doorknob as he approached his apartment.

Actually, his place was a one-room studio. *Greenville* sports editor Stan Faulkner's mother owned the place at the end of the driveway. The curvy drive wound past her house to an old red oak beside which the little house was conveniently tucked and shaded. It was definitely a throwback, furnished with a Murphy bed, kitchenette, and separate bath. At $75 a month, it was a steal. Fringe benefits included an occasional plate of fresh fried okra, tomatoes, mashed potatoes, and country fried chicken. It was like living next to your grandmother, the best landlord ever.

Wick knew before opening the envelope what surely must be inside. The number 86 flashed across his brain as well as a visual of that night at the Delta Epsilon house. He stepped inside the door, turned on the light, then sat down in his lone chair to open it.

"Greetings: You are hereby ordered for induction into the Armed Forces of the United States . . ." Included were details on when and where to appear for physical, psychological, mental, and moral evaluation. In Wick's case, he was still registered with the draft board back in Rome. He would report there with required documents, and his group would be bused to Atlanta for the listed evaluations.

The good news, Wick learned a couple days later, was that Secretary of Defense Melvin Laird had announced that the department would begin to draw down the number of troops currently serving in Vietnam. That scenario presented an option theretofore not available. If determined fit for service after all evaluations, one had thirty days to join a reserve unit within any branch of the military. With Wick's career in motion, the opportunity to join the reserves rather than active duty was good news indeed.

However, the major news in their timeline: Hollie and Wick were planning to wed in April. Joining the reserves was more than an option, it was a no-brainer!

The two had been back together for over six months, after sporadic dates and relationships with others proved to both they were truly meant for each other and made their love even stronger. On track to graduate early and with honors, Hollie was also contemplating an MBA degree, rare for a woman at the time. Wick's writing career could remain on track too, while he fulfilled his commitment to the military.

They could barely contain their excitement. Everything was falling into place!

After completing his physical and the requisite evaluations, Wick was cleared to search for a reserve unit in Greenville. Finding the Army Reserve had openings, Wick signed on in late November. All inductees, whether full-time army or reservists, had to go through boot camp, or BCT (basic combat training), which lasted eight weeks. Wick's paperwork was now in the processing pool, so he expected to learn his destination soon.

Commander Bowers believed Wick would likely be sent to either Fort Bliss in El Paso or Fort Polk in central Louisiana. In late December, Wick found out it would be neither. Fort Knox, just south of Louisville, Kentucky, was the army's choice for him. Wick was pleasantly surprised. The base was home to the Patton Museum, namesake of his favorite general, and also the site of the United States Bullion Depository, unequivocally the most secure and highly guarded facility on earth.

Wick hadn't exactly struck gold, but he much preferred Fort Knox over the heat in El Paso and the gnats and mosquitos in Louisiana.

His plane landed in Louisville on February 27. Before boarding in Atlanta, Wick had noticed three guys seated in the gate area whose conversation indicated they too were inductees. They all were from Corpus Christi, their government-issue tickets having routed them through Atlanta, and they were thirsty.

After exiting the plane, everyone had the same idea: Find a bar for one last cold beer before climbing on the bus over to Fort Knox.

Brady and Sid were tall, lean Texans, both with anxiety over soon giving up their cowboy boots for combat versions. Ezekiel, who was a ringer for Sergeant Garcia in the TV series *Zorro*, worried about the pounds the army would run off of his round torso. It was like last rites over a pitcher of beer.

Everybody made the bus, including several inductees waiting at the curb. All were delivered to the base and greeted by an imposing and vocal instructor. Suffice to say, the picnic was over for these civilians.

Wick's lingering concern was Saturday, April 28, the date scheduled for the wedding. Hollie and her mom had been busy with all the bookings and associated details, from A to Z.

Eight weeks of basic would be cutting it close, but Wick had no idea what was about to unfold.

The first few days of basic training were just that—handling the basics of conforming, molding young men into a unified unit. The recruits met for group sessions on the wearing and care of uniforms, making up bunks, dental and personal hygiene, protocol for saluting superior officers, assembly line vaccines, sanitation, nutrition, physical exercise, dexterity, and endurance. A big part of the latter was running, and the drill sergeants loved it, especially storming into the barracks at four thirty a.m. to rouse the sleeping subordinates for a two-mile run in the dark before breakfast.

One of the drill instructors relished the routine, running with his men, speeding up and falling back to keep the platoon in sync. Then after leading them back to the mess hall, he would pull out his pack of Winstons and light up. He told Wick he smoked two packs a day.

The most humbling unifier came while seated. The long assembly line moved about one inductee every minute. When it was your turn to step up into the chair, you closed your eyes so none of the falling locks would float into your eyes. Walking out the other end of the building, everyone rubbed their skinned head. When you put your Alaskan-style trapper hat back on, it didn't budge. George de Mestral, inventor of Velcro, would have been proud.

Inductees were bunked in the wooden barracks the first week. Because the buildings were so old and dry, platoon members were ordered to take turns every hour for fire watch overnight. The least flicker of flame could incinerate the structure. Of course, smoking was not allowed in any barracks.

All were moved into concrete barracks the second week. Wick's platoon was on the second floor. The bunks were newer and a little more comfortable, relatively speaking. The shining tile floors were to be kept that way, everyone working to do so as a team.

Individual bunks had to be made every morning, and when a drill sergeant strolled onto the floor, everyone was to stand at attention by their bunk.

On one occasion, the sternest and angriest sergeant showed up on an afternoon it had snowed. Everyone took their positions, except Johnson, a six-foot-two-inch slacker who was napping in his top bunk after lunch. The sergeant walked slowly up to the bunk and poked the inductee in the ribs, twice, but he didn't stir.

"Johnson, what the hell do you think you're doing?" the sergeant yelled into his ear. Johnson stirred but didn't get up.

"Get off that goddamned bed, now!" The sergeant began to tug at the mattress, then got a firm grip and began pulling it down. When Johnson realized the sergeant was really going to pull him off into the floor, he grabbed hold of the head bar, and the mattress dropped to the tiled concrete floor.

The enraged instructor, now pulling the mattress toward the outer wall, stopped to roll up one of the windows, then hoisted and pushed the bulky pallet through the opening like a marshmallow through the eye of a needle. The mattress fell to the snow-covered ground.

"Now you go get it if you want to sleep tonight. The next time I come through here during the day, your ass better not be on top of it!"

"Yes, sir" were the only two words that came out of Johnson's mouth while he stood as straight as his tall frame would allow.

You could have heard a pin drop as the sergeant exited the room.

The following week, after trying two younger inductees as platoon leader, the "runner" drill sergeant was not impressed and decided to make another change. While addressing the platoon in Monday morning formation, he walked down the line and stopped in front of Wick.

"Watters, you think you can lead these young men?"

"Yes sir, Sergeant!"

Wick stepped out of formation and marched to the front, doing an about-face beside the sergeant as instructed.

"Gentlemen, starting right now, Private Watters is your new platoon leader. In my absence, you will follow his lead. Any questions?" There was nothing but silence.

Later the sergeant pulled Wick aside, having looked over the paperwork and discovering his age. "You don't look twenty-three, private."

"Well, sir, I get that from a lot of my friends. Hopefully, someone will say the same thing when I'm eighty."

The sergeant actually laughed. "Let's get these young men in shape. Lead by example, Watters." The rest of the platoon were eighteen- and nineteen-year-olds. Wick's acquaintances from the airport had been placed in other platoons.

The next day, Wick had his first opportunity to lead. Before being dismissed from formation for dinner in the mess hall, the same sergeant challenged the platoon. "We're gonna find out how hungry you men really are. The last five men around the barracks to reach the front door will have to give me ten laps around the Patton Museum." Then he shouted, "Platoon, DISMISSED!"

Wick was off like a race horse, quickly took the lead, and held it until drawing near the long end of the barracks where he had to take a sharp right turn.

His torso was moving like the wind as his legs pumped harder than he thought was possible in combat boots. As if in a Sam Peckinpah movie, everything from his waist down shifted to slow gear, and then no gear. His legs told the rest of his body, "This is as far as we're going."

Suddenly, Wick was literally floating on air, with no control over his legs or feet. As he headed to the ground, he became a tumbling bowling pin, causing a chain reaction, taking out about ten soldiers behind him.

"You son of a bitch." "Asshole." "Prick." These were just a few of the invectives coming from the rear.

He managed to bounce up quickly, though, and made it around the building to the door—at least not in the last five.

Wick was embarrassed at first, then joined in the laughter with the rest of his platoon. He had led, but not by the best example. Because of the mishap, the sergeant removed the caveat for the last five.

Later in the mess hall, a voice from back in the food line shouted loud enough for everyone to hear, "Hey, Watters. Heard from your feet lately?"

The next week, after learning how to break down an M-16 assault rifle and strapping on a gas mask while subjected to real conditions in a test chamber, Wick was ready to decompress with a game of ping-pong. A recreation room, available to all BCT personnel after hours, was a short walk from the barracks.

He had played a pretty good game back in school but was a little rusty now. He watched as two inductees in their seventh week of basic went at it. They both were good, but the taller guy had a nasty serve and even nastier slap shot.

With the game over, Wick asked if he could take on the winner. They volleyed for a few minutes, then Wick nodded to the tall Asian American from Seattle that he was warmed up and ready to play.

The rust wore off early for Wick, and the two became more evenly matched. The tall player won the first two games, then Wick rallied to win the next two to even the match. The fifth and deciding game went to deuce, the pair having drawn a crowd by now. His opponent made it 12–11 and needed one more to close out the match. It was easy to see that these two were hypercompetitive.

Wicked saved himself on a couple of shots, flirting with the back line both times. The senior inductee anticipated a crossover backhand from Wick, who misfired, returning the ball with a high, fat margin that appeared to be the size of a softball by the time his opponent hit it.

Wick was on his heels awaiting a monster slap, which came at him so hard and fast he was defenseless, had no chance of returning the ball, and for sure didn't have time to get out of the way.

In a nanosecond the ball hit his right eye. It stung like a bee, especially since he was wearing a hard contact lens. He went to one knee and someone brought him a cold compress. His opponent immediately came over to apologize, but Wick told him one was not needed. It was a great shot, and Wick congratulated him on the win. Wick waited for the compress to ease the pain and pressure in his eye, then got up and returned to the barracks.

The accident presented a problem, however. Wick had no glasses with him for a backup. The prescription for his eyes was strong, and without them he was virtually blind. Protocol required army-issue glasses to advance through the rough exercises and drills ahead in basic.

Coincidentally, all inductees in his platoon were scheduled for eye exams the following Monday. Wick rested his right eye over the weekend and wore a contact lens in his left eye to at least give him monovision.

The right eye felt better on Monday morning, and Wick popped in his contact; no pain so far.

"The cornea in your right eye looks like it's been through a meat grinder. How did that happen?" the optometrist inquired as he shined the light across Wick's eye. Wick gave him the details.

"I'm going to refer you to a specialist at the base hospital. Give it another week to heal and we will call over to book you an appointment for the next Monday. Call this number before the weekend to confirm your time," he instructed, giving Wick a small tube of ointment to ward off any infection.

The next Monday morning at nine, Wick was in the chair again, this time with an ophthalmologist peering into his eye.

"Doesn't look like your cornea has healed much," said the doctor, who was about thirty. "Let's do an exam first so we can accurately evaluate your eye."

After completing his evaluation, the doctor sat down at a small built-in desk in the corner. "Were your eyes examined at your physical in Atlanta?"

"Yes and no. They told me to take out my contacts, then they looked at them through something similar to a microscope, but they never tested my eyes directly."

"I can't really write you the appropriate prescription until that cornea heals completely."

A light went off in Wick's head. "Doctor, if I miss another week and don't have a pair of army-issue glasses, I most likely will be recycled, have to rotate out of my group, and start the BCT process all over," Wick said with an urgency in his voice.

The doctor didn't respond but turned around and sat back down at his desk.

"What was the date of your physical in Atlanta?" He began writing. "What was your induction date? What is your birth date and age?" The doctor kept asking and writing.

He then stood up and told Wick he could get up from the exam chair.

"Take this out the door to the right, down the hallway to the next right, and then stop at the first door on the left. The lady there will know what to do, and you won't need to come back here. Keep your right contact out for at least a week to allow the cornea to heal fully."

Wick held the form close to his face to decipher it, which was difficult since his eyes had been dilated for the exam. It had been signed at the bottom left by the doctor. In the box to the right it read, "Unfit for induction. Medical discharge."

Wick turned and looked straight into the doctor's eyes, though his own were still a little fuzzy . . . but not so fuzzy he couldn't see the doctor smiling. Wick gave the man a firm handshake and thanked him for his professional evaluation.

He followed the directions down the hall to the office where a woman signed and stamped the form, giving him a copy and a smile.

Wick was ecstatic inside and humbled as he boarded the bus back to the barracks.

Years later he would reflect on the experience. When asked if he had served in the military, he would joke that he was a "ping-pong casualty."

The truth was he had been in the right place at the right time. It certainly helped that Melvin Laird had ended the draft in January and begun to draw down American troops in Vietnam, and the good doctor read the circumstances and made his assessment accordingly.

Wick reminded himself as he grew older, but for the grace of God, he was not called to war in a country and region where so many young men were in the wrong place at the wrong time. It was a guilt he would harbor for the rest of his life.

Exiting the military involved reversing all the paperwork that got a person to Fort Knox in the first place. Before he parted with his platoon and company, Wick said goodbye to a few inductees who had become buddies during the past five weeks, wishing them well and safe travels wherever their deployments might take them.

Separation would take a week. Wick was moved from his BCT barracks to one designated for discharges, an old barrack near the mess hall. Discharge categories were Honorable, General, Under Honorable Conditions, Under Other than Honorable Conditions, Bad Conduct, and Dishonorable. He was sharing space with misfits and malcontents, including suicidals and felons. He kept a watchful eye on the latter.

As example, the latrine was an open room with three rows of five toilets each. No privacy stalls were installed, which could enable someone to use or deliver drugs or do harm to themself.

Everyone was assigned a job, task, or chore, from mopping floors, cleaning latrines, digging trenches, or garbage collection. Wick volunteered for the garbage detail. At least he would be outdoors in fresh air, to the extent one could when hanging on the back of a garbage truck. It also allowed him to see more of Fort Knox than he would have during eight weeks of BCT. The humbling job reminded him how much he appreciated the crews back home who did this for a living, and how much he missed writing.

On his last day at Fort Knox, while walking back from the mess hall, he had an unexpected encounter. He still was not wearing his contacts, on doctor's orders.

Suddenly, an arm from behind grabbed Wick's left shoulder and spun him around.

"What's your name, son!" yelled the man.

"Wick Watters, sir," replied Wick, wondering what he had done wrong.

The officer moved in closer, his face about ten inches from Wick's.

"What do you see, Watters?"

Wick was perplexed. "I don't know, sir."

Frustrated, the man grabbed both Wick's shoulders and shook him vigorously. "What the hell do you see on my uniform?" he yelled again.

Wick's eyes rolled down the soldier's face to the uniform collar, where two parallel silver bars were affixed. *Holy shit, he's a captain!*

"Why didn't you salute when you passed me just now. Are you blind?"

Wick stepped back and gave a proper salute.

"Yes, sir. Right now I am. That's why I'm being medically discharged, sir, because of my vision. My right eye was injured, with a torn cornea." He inwardly prayed the man wouldn't asked him how. "The base doctor instructed me to keep my contacts out until I arrive home. I'm very sorry, sir."

The enlightened captain said nothing but simply shook his head and walked on.

Wick would hire a cab early Saturday morning for the Louisville airport and take the first flight to Atlanta. There Hollie would be waiting at the airport for the ride back to Rome.

He couldn't have been more content when the pilot announced, "Ladies and gentlemen, we have been cleared for landing."

Hollie, my parents, and Uncle Tom aren't going to believe this!

Chapter Sixteen

Oostanaula Vows

Wick's plane touched down at eleven a.m. With the flight maybe half full and only an overstuffed duffel bag stored overhead, Wick grabbed it and was off the plane and down the ramp in less than five minutes.

They made eye contact immediately, Hollie admiring Wick's buzz cut as he walked up, dropped his bag, and embraced her for a full minute. It wasn't like he was coming home from war or a long deployment, though Hollie was just as thankful as if he were.

They bypassed luggage claim and held hands all the way to the short-term parking lot, the latter somewhat poetic. Neither Wick nor Hollie had any idea when he left for Louisville over a month earlier just how short term it would be.

The doctor had given him a combination of disinfecting and numbing eye drops to use as needed, enabling Wick to take the wheel for the drive home. He navigated through the Atlanta traffic to give Hollie a break as she brought him up to date on the wedding plans.

"Mother and I have sent out 140 invitations, including to your colleagues in Greenville, college mates from both UGA and Berry, relatives and friends on the Watters and O'Hara sides, and of course vendors and grocers across the six southern states. Most all the details are checked off, from appetizers to wedding cakes to mints. Uncle Tom, bless his heart, assured me he will have enough stew prepared. Still, you should check with him to ensure he has enough help in and outside the kitchen." She paused to catch her breath.

"My goodness, Hollie, you've been busy while I've been protecting the gold at Fort Knox." He turned to her with a wink.

"I'm still letting it soak in, Wick. I was really worried with the run-up to eight weeks of BCT there might be a hitch somewhere. Now you're home, discharged, and separated from the reserves as well."

"We're blessed, sweetheart; no doubt about it."

Wick returned to the wedding to-do list. "I'll get on the phone Monday morning to confirm the tents, lighting, and band. Also, I need to check with Uncle Burton to assign a couple guys from the plant to handle parking at the farm."

"Who have you decided on for your best man?"

"I'm fortunate to have a bunch of close friends from high school and college—Lynn, Randy, Ronnie, Harold, John, Frank, and Doolin, and that's just O High. Wayne, Ken, Ralph, James, Tom, Mike, Larry, and Dan at UGA." Then he paused a few seconds.

"Uncle Tom, he's my best man, and long before you and I ever dreamed about a wedding. I'm going to drive over to tell him tonight."

"Wick," she teared up, "that's wonderful and so deserving. He's going to be so proud." She paused. "He's eighty-four now. Are you sure he's up to it physically, especially after cooking all the stew?"

"I understand your concern. The man is on a cane, but you let me handle it. I've already got a plan for that."

"How about the music? Who did you book before you left for Louisville?" Hollie awaited the surprise.

"A popular and diverse group called Night Train. An eight-piece band with a man and woman vocalist. They can play anything from the '50s right up to now, and yes, they have horns."

They both laughed out loud together. Hollie always asked if a band had a horn section. Wick had made sure Night Train included brass instruments in its repertoire.

They went silent for a few minutes. When Wick glanced over, Hollie was sound asleep. Rising early on a Saturday morning to drive to the Atlanta airport together with the excitement of him coming home had worn her down.

She slept the rest of the way home, probably even sounder once Wick got on the state highway and the back roads to the Oostanaula. Rome, home sweet Rome.

As soon as Wick turned into the long drive off Polaris Terrace, the dogs came barking. They sensed Wick was coming home too. Hollie awoke to their throaty barks. Raleigh and Edith were coming down the steps to greet them.

Edith got the first hug, as Raleigh waited his turn. Wick's father's bear hug felt good too.

"I know you must be tired," he acknowledged, "but do you feel like a game of ping-pong later?" Wick flashed a big smile with a thumbs up, but Edith wanted to know more about his eyes. He had driven home with his contacts in but was about to make a beeline for his room and a pair of glasses.

"I had no problem driving home, but I'm calling Doctor Anthony Monday morning for an appointment and new prescription." He found a pair of glasses in the back of his desk drawer, then Wick and Hollie sat down for an early dinner with Raleigh and Edith. She had prepared a plate of fresh garden vegetables with country fried steak for everyone, and especially for Wick, a generous slice of German chocolate cake, his favorite. After brushing his teeth and a quick kiss for Hollie, he was out the door to Uncle Tom's.

Tom was rocking away on his small deck, listening to the wildlife make music as the Oostanaula carried on. Wick had brought Uncle Tom something special from Fort Knox—a numbered, signed charcoal drawing of General George S. Patton by artist Jody Harmon. The likeness captured the general's stoic disposition, in combat uniform replete with medals and four stars, the latter on his helmet, both sides of his collar, and his epaulets.

Making it even more special, it was *the last* print, 992/1000. The artist had gifted the first eight prints to family and friends. Wick had held the frame in his lap the entire flight to Atlanta.

Wick walked around to the back side of the cabin and stopped below the steps.

"I'm looking for a Roman who's gone AWOL from Fort Knox. We have reason to believe he might be hiding here," he called out in a deep voice. Uncle Tom turned and pointed at Wick.

"You rascal you. Come up here and let me admire that haircut." The two bear-hugged, and Uncle Tom couldn't resist running his hand over Wick's GI coif.

They sat down as the now April breeze cooled the air. A few wild dogwoods across the river were flirting with blooms as the sun descended on the deck.

"You sure had a unique experience at Fort Knox. Who would've thought you would be discharged and home in plenty of time for the wedding. I've been keeping in touch with Hollie and your folks. Everyone is so excited, including me. I can't wait to see Hollie walk down the aisle, and you standing there so handsome awaiting such a beautiful bride."

With that, Wick jumped in. "We're super excited too, and so proud you will be there with us."

"I wouldn't miss it for the world," affirmed Uncle Tom as he patted Wick on the shoulder.

"I mean really *with* us. I've been blessed with many good, close friends from grade school to college, Uncle Tom. Most of them will be attending the wedding, but I want you to be standing beside me. I would be honored to have you as my best man."

Uncle Tom widened his eyes and opened his mouth, but nothing came out for a few seconds. "I would be humbled and so grateful, Wick, if you don't mind my cane joining me. I don't want to embarrass anyone by stumbling around at the altar."

"By all means, Uncle Tom. I'm probably going to be so nervous, I'll need one too."

They both laughed at that image.

"Before the sun goes down on us, I've got something in the car for you. I'll be right back."

Wick returned with the frame, wrapped in kraft paper and decorated with red, white, and blue ribbons. Uncle Tom carefully unwrapped the package after removing the patriotic ribbons. Once again, his eyes widened but his mouth could not speak as he admired the detailed drawing of Patton.

Wick gave him the story behind the artist and the good fortune of acquiring the very last print.

Uncle Tom was so impressed, he wanted Wick to come inside and find a place to hang it right then. Wick found a perfect space on the right side of the fireplace.

Uncle Tom thanked Wick, again and again, for choosing him best man. The two said good night, Tom ready for bed and Wick driving back home, content that he had made a wise man happy.

Wick's eye fully healed, and a new prescription for contact lenses and glasses was on the way. With less than three weeks until the wedding, he doubled back to make sure everything was on schedule operationally and logistically.

Three large white tents trimmed with strings of decorative twenty-five-watt bulbs would be staked parallel to the river. The band would set up on the large oak deck already there. Three bartenders behind mobile bars would be conveniently positioned near each tent. Separate buffets centered and surrounded by table and chairs would begin serving fifteen minutes after the ceremony was over, and it would begin at five o'clock. Night Train would begin playing for the bride and groom dance at seven p.m., and then the floor would open for all.

A violin trio and jazz combo would alternate with light music an hour before the wedding.

Wick was having a sixty- by six-foot walkway covered with red carpet installed for the wedding party, with seventy-five chairs set up on each side. A custom rail would be installed in the spot where Wick and Uncle Tom would be standing. Uncle Burton had rented two covered, double-seated passenger carts for the two valets, Sam and Dave, fraternity brothers from UGA, to transport seniors or anyone needing a ride from the parking area to the wedding venue.

The day had finally come—Saturday, April 28, 1973.

All systems were a go as far as Hollie and Wick were concerned. Every single box had been checked and rechecked. The weather forecast was perfect for late April: mostly sunny with no chance of rain, a temperature at five p.m. around seventy-two degrees, accompanied by a five mph wind. A slight breeze off the Oostanaula was always appreciated.

Most of the attendees arrived by four, and the Brunswick stew had been delivered. The venerable stew master and best man were content.

By five o'clock sharp everyone had been seated while the strings added music to the late afternoon breeze.

The bride's and groom's mothers had been seated.

Wick had Uncle Tom holding on to his right arm while the cane steadied the proud Cherokee on his right. He was so sharp in his tuxedo and tie. No hat today, though.

They made the sixty-foot stroll without a hitch, and Uncle Tom had no trouble turning around in front of the short rail, which he leaned against slightly. Wick had ensured there were enough braces and screws in the treated posts to steady a bull.

The strings began to play the traditional "Bridal Chorus" or march as Buddy O'Hara walked his oldest daughter down the aisle. *She's so poised and beautiful,* thought Wick as his knees began to weaken just a tad. Thank goodness he had made the rail wide enough for both him and Uncle Tom.

The closer Hollie came, the more his heart thanked his brain. He was about to marry his typing and Bahama Blue buddy. She was the most complete woman he would ever know and love.

After Buddy kissed his daughter and stepped back to give her away, Wick and Hollie drew closer.

The minister, also a Delta Ep, recited relevant passages from the Bible for the couple's benefit, then turned to Wick and Hollie as they repeated the traditional and sacred vows of marriage.

Each happily answered the minister with the two words that would punctuate a lifetime of devotion, love and partnership . . . "I do."

After pronouncing them man and wife, Reverend Barry Ellis granted Wick the pleasure of kissing his new bride. The minister then presented Mr. and Mrs. Coleman Brunswick Watters.

Their honeymoon in the Canadian Rockies allowed Wick and Hollie plenty of time for reflection and an eye toward the future.

Hollie had graduated early with her BBA in business and was excited to pursue an MBA, which Berry College now offered. Wick's job had been held for him at the *Greenville News,* and he wanted to continue gaining as much writing experience as possible. They agreed that now was the time, with no children, to make the most of the next year. Hollie would remain in Rome to work on her masters, while Wick would keep his studio in Greenville and rejoin the newspaper. He would commute to Rome on weekends.

After another year at the *Greenville News* following his stint at Fort Knox, the commutes to Rome became taxing. Faulkner had made it a little easier for the couple by scheduling most of Wick's assignments during the week so he and Hollie could be together on the weekends. The thoughtful exception wasn't something for which Wick had lobbied, yet he much appreciated it. Wick was uncomfortable when he delivered the news to his boss: He was moving back to Rome.

Faulkner was disappointed to lose Wick, yes, but he was equally sympathetic and appreciated the Watters's situation. The entire sports staff plus Rupe met at Baka's tavern after Wick's last night at the paper. He enjoyed hearing Stan's and Rupe's stories from the good ole days, plus those recounted by the current staff. Of course, the evening wouldn't have been complete without one last dance from maestro Baka. Everyone clapped to the beat as they joined the animated "Greek Streak" in the traditional Kalamatianos.

When he walked out of the tavern into the night air, Wick looked across the street where the old city hall once stood. It had been stubborn to the end giving up its space, but the new city hall shined now in the Main Street lights and would be bustling tomorrow, a beacon for Greenville's growth, which in just a decade would attract BMW, Michelin, and related industries. Downtown would be infused with a European influence that would spawn fine dining restaurants, cafés, theatres, and cultural events.

Edith had arranged for Wick to come to the Rome *News-Tribune* office to meet with the publisher, Baird Mahoney. He was open to discussing opportunities the newspaper was considering and any ideas Wick had that might align with those. Though the circulation of the paper, at 48,000, was considerably less than the *Greenville News,* the press was growing, had built new offices, and had installed a new web press.

After reviewing Wick's resume and clippings from the *Greenville News,* and with Wick emphasizing his desire to write features and human-interest pieces, Mahoney revealed that the paper's longtime sports editor, Von Riggins, would be retiring at the end of July.

Mahoney's phone then buzzed, his secretary confirming that Congressman Davis was on line two.

"Excuse me, Wick. I need to take this call."

"Would you like me to step out, sir?" Wick offered.

Mahoney shook his head, holding up his right hand as if to stop traffic.

The publisher and congressman spoke for about ten minutes as Wick made notes in his reporter's notebook and glanced around Mahoney's mahogany walls, covered with awards, citations, and photos taken with celebrities and politicians. Most notable was the frame with Mahoney and legendary Alabama football coach Paul "Bear" Bryant. Each had one arm around the other's shoulder. Edith had reminded him the two were "good friends" and Bama alums.

As soon as the call ended, Mahoney returned the phone to its cradle while declaring, "Wick, I'll hire you as our new sports editor, effective July first."

A surprised but pensive Watters adjusted his posture in the winged chair he had occupied for some thirty minutes.

"Mr. Mahoney, I sincerely appreciate your offer. I really do. Sportswriting has been a great experience and a real proving ground for me. I've met people and traveled places I likely never would have but for the opportunity Stan Faulkner gave me, and I've developed a writing style driven by a curiosity which I believe will serve me well as I transition to feature writing.

"That said, does the Rome *News* have any opportunities now, or any you are considering?"

Mahoney went silent for a few seconds, pinching his chin with a thumb and index finger. "Wick, I'm sorry to say no, not at this time. Reason is, as you saw when you parked in our lot, this is a new building—from offices, to departments . . . all the way to the press. Our expenditure, that is to say our investment, has been substantial.

"I think you would be perfect to succeed Riggins, but you've made it clear feature writing is your pursuit. Unfortunately, our staff and payroll are maxed out right now, with no room to create any new positions. Perhaps down the road, say six months to a year? If you're still available then or things aren't going as well as expected where you land, please give me a call."

Chapter Seventeen

Lewis

Wick wore his light gray suit and favorite scarlet red paisley tie. He had hand-shined his black wingtips the night before, though misjudging the high curb at 72 Marietta Street now rendered a slight scuff on his right shoe. *So what. Is anyone really going to notice or care?*

He was rolling the dice. He had no appointment at the *Atlanta Journal Constitution*—only a name or two to drop as he walked into the lobby and up three steps to the security guard kiosk.

"Is there anyone in the sports department, sir? My name is Wick Watters. Wilt Downing with the Atlanta Falcons and Hank Bremen of the *Greenville News* referred me here."

The guard picked up the phone and repeated what he could remember to someone upstairs as Wick and his red notebook of clippings waited.

"Yes, he's standing right here," said the guard to the person on the line. "Okay, right, I'll send him up now." The man handed

Wick a clip-on visitor tag and motioned to the elevators around the right corner. "Stop at the fifth floor."

On the elevator ride up, flashbacks convinced him more than ever he would rather take a part-time job here, if available, than make a commitment to a job in a smaller market that he knew wouldn't be the right path for him. This would give him time to continue seeking a feature writer position, preferably with a national magazine.

The elevator doors parted, and immediately the smell of glue pots converged on Wick's nostrils. The pungent yet nostalgic smell was the *Greenville News* times two.

He was stepping into the sports departments for the *Journal and Constitution,* the afternoon and morning editions. The entire floor appeared empty and quiet, no typewriters banging or teletypes ticking. Wick had become accustomed to the latter, which sounded much like the reverberations made by Mama Watters's old Singer treadle, a comforting resonance to Wick.

He spotted only one person, sitting at a desk to the far left. The man was editing copy while extinguishing a Marlboro in a brimming ashtray.

"Come on over, Wick. You caught me at a good time, before all the chaos begins," said Lewis Grizzard.

By that time, 1973, Grizzard had been the executive sports editor of the *Atlanta Journal* for nearly four years. Jim Minter, *Journal* executive editor, was obviously impressed with his talent and experience, hiring Grizzard with that title at only twenty-three, the youngest ever for the paper. He would soon be lured away by the *Chicago Sun Times* as its executive sports editor, then return to Atlanta in 1977 as a popular humor/human interest columnist.

Grizzard became syndicated in over 450 newspapers, which led to twenty-five books, eighteen making the *New York Times* Best Seller list.

Wick immediately realized the magnitude—sheer luck—of this impromptu interview.

"I had no idea the guard downstairs was speaking to you when I asked if there was anyone in sports. It's a pleasure to meet you, Lewis," began Wick, in awe, believing at three and a half years younger he could address the executive sports editor by his first name.

"So, you know Wilt with the Falcons?"

"Yes, sir, I do. The newspaper would send me out to Furman most days during camp to generate player interviews and updates. Wilt introduced me to several players—Claude Humphrey, John Zook, Joe Profit, Ken Burrow, to name a few, and of course Coach Van Brocklin."

After a brief conversation on Wick's background and experience, Lewis asked to see Wick's notebook of writing samples. As he flipped through the *Greenville News* clippings, Grizzard noted that he and Hank Bremen had crossed paths when Lewis was at UGA (his alma mater too). Hank and Lewis were both vying for the "spotter" job in the broadcast booth for Bulldog games. Bremen got the nod, and Lewis wound up seizing an opportunity to join Chuck Perry at the new, independent *Athens Daily News,* competition for the *Athens Banner Herald.*

Ironically, Perry, at the *Banner Herald* in 1972, had given Wick his first byline when a senior journalism student at UGA. It was a fluff piece interpreting the lingo used by servers and curb hops at the popular Varsity fast food restaurant. Perry liked it enough to position it on the front page, which of course was fine by Wick.

"Okay, Wick. Sit down at any of those typewriters behind you and knock out a lead based on this breaking news: Vince Dooley has announced he is leaving the University of Georgia to take a head coaching job in the NFL with the Cincinnati Bengals. You've got fifteen minutes."

Lewis then handed him some copy paper.

Under normal circumstances this would have been an elementary task, but suddenly it became much bigger than that: an opportunity for Wick to get his foot in the door to more possibilities down the road.

Don't screw it up, Wick.

He sat down behind one of the new IBM roller ball typewriters, a new machine to him. Not what his fingers or typing rhythm were used to, but he could manage. It was all about the content, getting it right and ready in the allotted time.

With a little perspiration surfacing on his forehead and reminding himself this was a fictional lead, Wick hammered out six paragraphs. He had included all the pertinent details he believed supported such an important lead. When he stood up to walk the copy over, he hoped his active stomach wasn't audible across the spacious room, which was still empty except for the two.

Wick waited patiently as Lewis read through the extemporaneous exercise, making a couple marks with his pencil.

"Looks good, Wick. Just one correction. Dooley indeed was the youngest head coach when hired at Georgia, but he was thirty-one, not thirty-three."

Lewis liked what he saw but confirmed to Wick (as expected) that there were no full-time positions on the staff. However, he could use him Friday nights and Saturdays on the rim, writing headlines and short leads.

"That works for me, Lewis. I appreciate your taking time for me this afternoon, and look forward to being on board this Friday night."

With that, the two shook hands. Wick was officially on the payroll of the *Atlanta Journal Constitution,* a major metropolitan newspaper that had a rich history since its founding in 1868.

As Wick stood in front of the elevator to go down, he thought about how fortunate he was.

Hollie's not going to believe this, and Uncle Tom? He'll be so content.

Wick was fortunate to have a fraternity brother, Wayne Westin, who had an apartment on the north side of town. Wick would drive to Atlanta on Friday afternoons for work at the *Journal* that evening, stay overnight at Westin's, then drive back to the *AJC* for a long Saturday, returning to Rome that evening.

On his fifth weekend at the *Journal,* Saturday, September 29, 1973, the phones were ringing more than usual that evening. It was the Atlanta Braves' next to last game of the season, at home against the Houston Astros. Hank Aaron, in pursuit of Babe Ruth's long-standing record of 714 home runs in a season, was on the verge of reaching and breaking that long, evasive record.

Hammering Hank drove the pitch from the Astros' Jerry Reuss over the centerfield wall for number 713. The phones really began to light up now. With one more game tomorrow, would Aaron tie the record at season's end?

Wick fielded his share of calls, from questions about Aaron's bat to who would be pitching on Sunday, all positive. Only a couple that Wick took were negative. The first questioned Aaron's legitimacy should he eclipse Ruth's 714, because Hank had a longer season, 162 games to do so.

Wick debunked this assertion. Roger Maris of the New York Yankees had similar detractors who evoked the asterisk because Maris's record sixty-one home runs in 1961 were across 162 games. The Bambino had hit his sixty home runs in a shorter, 154-game season.

You can't argue with a turnip, thought Wick.

The most disturbing call came from an inebriated woman, crying through her protestation that it would be "un-American" for Aaron to break Babe Ruth's record. Wick ended the nonsense by simply cradling the phone.

The following season in Atlanta, on April 8, 1974, Aaron broke Ruth's record, hitting number 715 off Al Downing of the Los Angeles Dodgers. He finished his twenty-three-year career with a total 755 homers, a record that stood for another thirty-three years.

How's that for legitimacy?

In late September, Wick got a call from a former colleague at the *Greenville News* who knew he was looking for an opportunity as a feature writer.

"Wick, I was speaking to Cally Gault yesterday, and he mentioned an alumnus in Atlanta with a publishing company with several magazines. Maybe it's worth giving him a call?"

Gault was head football coach at Presbyterian College in Clinton, South Carolina. Wick had covered several PC games and Cally's weekly press conferences. The team was nicknamed the "Blue Hose," celebrating the unique socks worn by the football team in the early 1900s.

Hamilton "Ham" Edson, a 1962 graduate of Presbyterian, was editor of *Sports Dealer News,* one of fourteen business-to-business magazines owned by W.R.J. MacCallan Publishing.

"I understand you're an alum of Presbyterian? I spent two years covering that neck of the woods with the *Greenville News.* Cally Gault and the Blue Hose were part of my itinerary. A fine coach and mentor with a great culture of overachievers," Wick began the conversation.

"Thank you. It's always nice to hear good things about one's alma mater. I have a lot of respect for Cally too," returned Edson.

Wick explained that Coach Gault had mentioned Ham's name in a conversation with a former colleague at the paper. By chance did the company have any openings for a feature writer?

"Well, that's interesting and timely. I just came out of a management meeting, and we are seriously considering venturing outside our comfort zone. All fourteen of our titles are trade publications across several industries, from textiles, automotive, building, hardware, design, construction, and grocery to sporting goods."

"Exactly what market are you looking at?" inquired Wick.

"One focused on people, leadership, and lifestyle," offered Edson.

"I would be very interested in discussing that venture with you in person, Ham. Would that be possible sometime next week?"

"Let me put you on hold for a couple minutes, Wick, while I look at my calendar and make a quick call internally."

Wick held for nearly three minutes before Edson came back on the line.

"How about next Tuesday morning at nine thirty? Our president and CEO, Franklin Felton, will be joining us. We're located at 1670 Peachtree."

"Sounds great, Ham. I look forward to meeting you both. Have a good weekend."

Their meeting couldn't have gone better. The publication title would be *American Leader,* edited for the general audience, a national monthly glossy magazine sold by subscription only and supported by an elaborate media campaign—radio and print. As sales progressed, a TV campaign would be considered as well. The company would hire talent from perceived competitive pubs, and two major investors would ensure the new magazine had the necessary resources and network to be successful.

Both Felton, Edson, and the board agreed that Coleman Brunswick Watters would be their first hire as editor-at-large, traveling anywhere in the country to secure interviews and cover stories with America's best leaders.

Hollie's not going to believe this. Uncle Tom will be beyond contented.

Wick had been at the *AJC* for only six weeks, but he had now found the opportunity he had been seeking. If not for his time at the newspaper and driving back and forth to Rome, he would have been stir-crazy. Now he could make plans. Wick and Hollie would rent an apartment or house near downtown Atlanta. The farm would be their retreat, and Uncle Tom, at eighty-four but still in good health for his age, would continue to oversee the landscape, though Burton would definitely keep one eye on him.

It was mutual therapy. Uncle Tom breathed life into the farm, and the farm breathed life into him.

Lewis was pleased to hear Wick had landed the opportunity he had been searching for and wished him well, but it wasn't goodbye. A few times over the years, he and Wick would coincidentally cross paths.

Wick was in his office a year later working on an interview with a CEO out in Riverside, California, when a call came in from the publisher at the *Ledger-Enquirer,* Randy McKenzie.

"Hello, Wick. I'll be brief. I'm looking for a new sports editor over here in Columbus, and Lewis Grizzard suggested I contact you."

"Thank you, Mr. McKenzie. I'm flattered and appreciate Lewis thinking of me, but I have to say I'm very content where I am now."

"I completely understand, but when Lewis offers up a name or recommendation, I'm definitely going to follow through. If you ever get over to Columbus, please give me a call and let's have lunch."

"I sure will, Mr. McKenzie. Have a good day now."

Wick smiled as he put down the phone.

I am certainly low on his totem pole, but for Lewis to remember me, much less recommend me? Now that's class.

The second encounter came on December 2, 1978. Through a contact at WSB-TV in Atlanta, Wick was able to secure two press passes for the annual Georgia vs. Georgia Tech game. The archrivals would face off in Athens, the Bulldogs ranked just outside of the Top Ten at #11. It turned out to be perhaps the most exciting game for alumni and spectators in the history of the rivalry.

Wick wanted to surprise his father just before the game with the press passes. The ladies were back home shopping, so everybody was content, including the young couple to whom Wick gave his regular pair of tickets.

After announcing to Raleigh where they were sitting, he reminded him they would be situated among the "working press," so the two would have to check their emotions at the door. Any animated behavior or excessive celebration might prompt security to escort them out of the press box and lounge, especially with ABC sportscaster Al Michaels doing the play-by-play just twenty feet to their right.

For "cover," father and son wore cameras around their necks, though Raleigh had no film in his 35mm Minolta. Wick donned his regular Canon, equipped with a zoom lens. With their green press passes dangling from their pockets, at least they looked the part.

While they were standing in the middle of the press lounge, over walked Lewis.

"How's it going, Wick?"

"Well, I'll be. Lewis Grizzard. It's great to see you again," said Wick, turning toward his dad. "Lewis, this is my father, Raleigh."

"Nice to meet you Mr. Watters. Looks like you two are ready for some photo journalism."

Wick laughed. "Hopefully we don't get tossed out. We're under disguise as the 'working press.'"

Lewis laughed too, understanding the covert operation.

The two muzzled fans were excruciatingly challenged in the first half. Underdog Tech shocked everyone by taking a 20–0 lead over the Bulldogs. Were it not for a late Georgia touchdown just before the half, the Yellow Jackets would have skunked the home team going into the locker room. By the time the two teams came out for the second half, Wick had already decided they would have to join in with the other fifty-five thousand UGA fans to bring Georgia back. When Dooley's Dogs began to score, the din in

Sanford Stadium grew louder. In fact, ABC later confirmed it was the loudest they had ever registered for an open-air stadium.

The strategy was, if they were going to be thrown out, Raleigh and Wick might as well get a head start.

By the time Georgia rallied to an unbelievable 29–28 victory, the two paparazzi to the left of Al Michaels had exhausted their repertoire of high fives, chest bumps, vertical leaps, first down, and touchdown signals.

It would be fifteen years before Wick would bump into Lewis again. Wick had just gotten off the underground tram at Hartsfield International Airport in Atlanta, heading over to the concourse and gate for his flight to Texas, when he recognized a figure moving toward him.

Just like that day when stepping off the elevator at the *AJC*, the concourse was empty and unusually quiet. It was a Sunday morning in the summer of 1993.

Lewis seemed a little feeble, but the patented glance over his glasses and that smile signaled a little mischief was well intact.

"Well, hello, Wick. Where you headed?"

"Out to San Antonio, Lewis. It's so good to see you. It's been awhile."

"Yes, yes. It has."

"Where are you coming in from?"

"Orlando. I like it down there."

Lewis glanced ahead, then turned around and peered behind him down the vacant walkway.

"Do you know how to get out of here, Wick?"

"Sure, Lewis. You want to keep walking in the same direction you are headed. That will put you on the escalators to baggage claim and the exit doors to the courtesy buses that will take you to the parking lots, or MARTA if you're taking it."

"Thanks, Wick. I do appreciate it. So, are you still writing?"

"I am, but I'm on the B2B side of publishing now. Who knows, one day, maybe when I'm retired, I'll write a book."

"That sounds great. When you do, send me a copy. I'd love to read it."

"I absolutely will, Lewis," affirmed Wick. "By the way, I'm forever grateful for the opportunity you gave me at the *AJC*. I was fortunate to be in the right place at the right time, face-to-face with one of the best writers and storytellers of our time."

"You're mighty kind, Wick. Mighty kind."

The two shook hands, then the Son of the South turned to make his way home.

Lewis Grizzard, forty-seven, died on March 20, the first day of spring 1994 after undergoing his fourth heart valve surgery. Complications caused a blood clot to settle in his brain, depriving it of oxygen. For those who enjoyed his humor, columns, and books, their breaths were taken away too.

Chapter Eighteen

Catfish

Lewis Grizzard's beloved black Labrador preceded him in death on Thanksgiving night, 1993, just four months before Grizzard's passing. The veterinarian said the dog's heart "gave out."

Three days after Lewis passed, Wick sent this letter to the editor of the *AJC*.

> I'm not sure why Lewis named me Catfish. Maybe because it sounds so southern. They tell me there's nothing more mouthwatering than a plate of the fish deep-fried. I wouldn't know. I prefer cheeseburgers and chili.
>
> "Cat," after all, is not something one would ordinarily name a dog, but then "bull" is an interesting name to hang on a dog too. Whatever his reason, I've always been sure of one thing. Lewis loved me. Maybe I was the son he never had? Or that I was a special gift from the legendary head coach Vince Dooley and wife Barbara?

Lewis and I indeed were as thick as Uncle Tom's Brunswick stew. Come January, we would have been together for 12 years. Not bad, considering his longevity with women. Lewis's marriages were the source of many humorous anecdotes in his books. All of us who shared a laugh or life with Lewis were better for it.

He was always forgiving, even after the golf balls, TV remotes, shoes, and glasses I mangled in the early years. He said I grew out of it at three. After that, I just grew. As I advanced to the status of "man's best friend," Lewis awarded me my space on the wonderful green couch, right next to him.

As his health began to decline, we watched many a Braves game, old Gary Cooper movie, Justin Wilson Cajun-cooking episode, or an A&E dig in Argentina ... you name it. With 50 cable channels we became five-star couch potatoes. Lazy times on the front porch were special too. Lewis liked to rock, and I liked to roll over and sleep.

All the heart surgeries had taken a toll on his body, but not his mind. His gift for telling a good story or wit for a quick line never waned. I missed those times, and riding in the truck too. We were Butch Cassidy and the Sundance Kid.

Then I up and died. Did dogs go to heaven? And if I made it, would it be Saint Peter or Bernard greeting me at the gates?

After that last stroke of Lewis's hand between my ears, my spirit was lifted up, drifting and floating through the clouds with a cool breeze passing over me. Colors of the rainbow began to light up the sky, and a burst of pure white covered my eyes as I began to be pulled up a beautiful stairway of pearl. At the top stood Saint Peter.

"So, you were Lewis Grizzard's dog?" he asked.

I bowed my head, thinking ... Does he mean that's a good thing?

"He makes me laugh too," reassured Saint Peter, "but your master is living on borrowed time."

Lewis had prayed the inevitable and, come late March, imminent surgery would be successful. He was hopeful even that he could make it to one more Masters in Augusta that April.

Just four months after my passing, I looked down on Georgia. The azaleas and dogwoods were beginning to bloom as Lewis died of a broken heart on the first day of spring.

"Go to him, Catfish," said Saint Peter from our porch in paradise, an empty rocker beside him.

"There he comes over the celestial horizon."

I leapt from the porch and ran toward the glow headed my way.

Lewis is alive, and I don't feel so bad myself!

Sincerely,
Catfish

Chapter Nineteen

Sequoyah's Spirits

Now, in the early spring of 1982, Hollie and Wick, along with everyone who admired the man, were deeply concerned about Uncle Tom. At ninety-two, Tom's health was in steady decline.

Uncle Burton had long since hired a full-time caretaker for the feeble Prophett, calling the lady "help." Miss Hattie had worked for the Watters family off and on for nearly fifteen years. At first Uncle Tom resisted. He was never one to complain, yet he knew his days on the Oostanaula farm were winding down.

A heavy rain shower pelted the river, creating a chill in the air. Wick had started a small fire for Uncle Tom in his cozy cabin. He and Hollie were seated on the hearth near the Cherokee, the firelight reflecting off his stoic face.

"I know death is near," he told the two, his glistening eyes fixed on the fire.

"Uncle Tom, please don't say that. We've got so many days together ahead of us," Hollie's voice encouraged, though breaking a bit.

"She's right, Uncle Tom," affirmed Wick, swallowing the lump in his throat. "You've got a birthday coming in September, and we're planning a big celebration with the family here on the river."

Tom's eyes remained fixed on the fire, its flames dancing higher.

"The spirits tell me otherwise, my beloved friends."

Wick and Hollie were holding hands now, hers gripping his tightly.

"I've led a good life, been blessed is so many ways. The Watters family, your grandfather Reed and grandmother Rose, so kind and supportive. Your parents, Raleigh and Edith, equally so. Your children, Joseph and Marie, I've loved as if my own. The friends I've made through the business and the farm. The joy of seeing you two fall in love, make your way through this sometimes crazy world. Raising a beautiful family of your own. Both wonderful, talented children. Wick, your career as a writer so rewarding, and Hollie so smart, dedicated, and devoted. You two were made for one another. I knew it the first time I saw you together.

"The same way I felt the first time I laid eyes on my sweet Aiyana. She has remained in my heart for now seventy-six years. She's spoken to me in so many ways, always through my heart so my head could follow."

The fire was beginning to die down, but not Uncle Tom's resolve.

"I am requesting, and would be honored, if you both would see I have a burial which respects Cherokee traditions. There's a book in the night table by my bed that details the protocol and rituals true to my heritage. I have a copy of my will in an envelope bearing your names inside that book. It assures funeral expenses will be distributed from my estate. Would you do that for Uncle Tom please?"

Hollie and Wick stood up, with eyes welled up, approached the man who had been an integral part of *their* life, and wrapped their arms tightly around him. No words were necessary.

They would abide and ensure Thomas Sequoyah Prophett was given the proper Cherokee burial he so richly deserved.

Over the next three weeks, Hollie made phone calls to those entities or institutions that could help pull all the elements together to enable an appropriate Cherokee funeral. She and Wick spoke on the phone every night wherever he was traveling to make sure they were in sync and understood all the recommendations being made.

Culturally, Cherokee Indians were very spiritual. They interpreted death as a transition to another place, not necessarily an end to this world. Tradition was for interment in the ground, believing that the body would nourish the earth. They were not embalmed nor were organs removed for donation.

Hollie was pleased when she called the local Jennings Funeral Home and learned they in fact were familiar with Cherokee protocol, having handled a couple in recent years.

Still, a Cherokee shaman was needed to conduct the service. For this, Hollie contacted the Tribal Council of the Cherokee Nation, headquartered in Tahlequah, Oklahoma, also deemed its capital. She learned quite a lot in her phone conversation with the spokesman for Principal Chief Moss Settler.

A majority of Cherokees practice Christianity, most as Baptists or Methodists. Converts believed this would improve their status and create opportunities for education and work for their families.

Ancient traditions included a reverence for the Great Spirit, in Cherokee known as *Unetlanvhi*. He presides over all things and created earth, is omnipotent, omnipresent, and omniscient. He made the earth to provide for children.

From a religious perspective, "We believe our Native traditions affirm the presence of God, our need for the right relationship with our Creator and the world around us, and a call for holy living," the spokesman told Hollie. "All souls after death continue to live on as spirits, some manifested into the bodies of animals while others unseen."

Ancient Cherokees even had a prayer for the Deer God. These animals were important to tribes for meat, clothing, tools, ceremonial accessories, and means of trade. The intent was to not hunt the animals down unmercifully, and that the Deer God not be angry with them.

"Deer God: We only kill what is needed for our families, and we are sorry."

Cedar, used to carry the honored dead, was also sacred to the Cherokee, as were the owl and cougar. Owls were admired, the screech species in particular, because of their eyes. Positioned on the front of their heads, they were perceived messengers of future events. The Cherokee learned hunting skills from the cougar.

Red and white colors were important, symbolically distinguishing supreme war chiefs (red) from supreme peace chiefs (white) among the Cherokee tribes.

The spokesman walked Hollie through the preparation for a Cherokee burial.

"The body is first washed and scented with lavender oil. Cherokees believe lavender has intense spiritual properties, of which are the cleansing of all impurities. The body is then wrapped in a white cotton sheet before being placed in the coffin. An eagle feather is positioned on the body because the eagle is revered by the Cherokee, and as well by most native American tribes.

"Cherokee prayers, led by the shaman, begin the funeral. He

prays for the deceased and provides spiritual lessons for the living. He delivers an ending prayer, and the body is carried to the designated resting place on the shoulders of the procession. Tradition calls for burial on the day of or day after death, but Mr. Prophett's funeral can be delayed given the circumstances." Hollie was relieved to hear this.

"Traditional Cherokee burials call for a seven-day mourning period under the auspices of the shaman." Hollie gasped when he said this.

"This period is considered a spiritual cleansing time for the survivors to be spiritually cleansed. During this time, family members are not allowed to be angry or jovial and must restrict their intake of food and water." Another gasp from Hollie.

"The shaman ritually cleanses the house with tea and removes any items deemed unclean from the house of the deceased." She gasped again.

"Following seven days of cleansing, the shaman takes the mourners to a river and instructs them to immerse themselves in water seven times, alternating their direction of facing east and west. After the immersing ceremony, the mourners are presented with fresh clothes, an offering of tobacco, and sanctified beads. After the end of the ceremony the mourners are welcomed back to the tribe."

Was this the last gasp?

The spokesman paused for Hollie to catch her breath.

"Mrs. Watters, please don't worry. The Cherokee Nation fully understands and respects your circumstances and will modify the protocol to adapt to your situation while keeping with the integrity and symbolic rituals of the services."

Hollie wished he had said that at the beginning. Wick was flying home that night, and they would discuss the details.

Hollie had relayed all of her conversation to the funeral home in Rome by the time Wick arrived. Sitting down with a cup of coffee in his comfortable winged chair, he listened to every detail Hollie had amassed from her conversation with Mr. Settler's spokesman.

Wick didn't hesitate. "Let's do it, Hollie. I love this man as much as my own father and grandfather. In fact, what do you think about adding to the ceremony?"

"Exactly how would we do that, Wick?" Hollie left off the gasp.

"Call the Tribal Council back and ask if they would agree to have, in addition to our securing the shaman, the principal chiefs of all three tribes present, one for each of our rivers. The Watters family would cover their airfare, and we would put them up at the farm. How's that for symbolism?"

"What a great idea! One question, though. Exactly who's going to be immersed in the Oostanaula?"

Wick laughed. "You and me, baby. The water might be a tad chilly, yes. We will wear a harness with a thick rope tethered to the dock so we can step out far enough to immerse but not too far, in case the river current is fast that day."

"How about the shaman?"

"I assume he will be standing on the bank or maybe the dock. You've worked hard on pulling this together, Hollie. Let's look back after this day comes with the peace of mind that our family has done our best for Uncle Tom, just as he has for the Watters."

"Yes, let's do it for Uncle Tom," Hollie said softly. She prayed the sweet man would make it to celebrate his birthday.

That day was coming sooner than anyone thought, except maybe Doctor Whitaker. Uncle Tom had been placed in the "failure to thrive" category. His mind remained clear, but his organs had slowly begun to shut down.

It was a partly sunny June morning when Doctor Whitaker examined Uncle Tom. He walked out onto the cabin deck where Wick stood, looking out on the river that had brought Papa Reed and Uncle Tom together as young boys so many years ago.

"I'm sorry, Wick. His decline has accelerated. You should contact Hollie and the family, let them know his passing is imminent."

Wick put one hand on the doctor's shoulder and thanked him for all he had done for the honorable man, then he stuck his head in the door to tell Miss Hattie he was calling Hollie to have her drive in from Atlanta. He first hesitated, then decided to step in Uncle Tom's bedroom one more time.

The Cherokee was asleep and appeared to be at peace. As soon as Hollie arrived, they would return to Uncle Tom's cabin and keep vigil. Other members of the Watters family would visit through the evening too, one more time.

The sad thing was that no one from the Prophett family would be joining in. Tom's parents had passed years earlier, and he had no brothers or sisters, no cousins, and no other family remaining.

On Sunday, June 13, 1982, at 2:28 a.m., Uncle Tom passed away, three months shy of his ninety-third birthday. Wick and Hollie were at his side, blessed to have learned so much from this selfless, loving man, and now prepared for his body and spirit to be transitioned honorably by the Tribal Council of the Cherokee Nation.

Services would be held at the Watters family farm on Wednesday, June 16, 1982, at two o'clock p.m., with burial on the banks of the Oostanaula River.

Uncle Burton dispatched a driver in a company van to pick up the three principal chiefs at the Atlanta airport on Tuesday afternoon. Harland stood near the entry to baggage claim, like the professional limo drivers, holding up an identifying sign. His read "Sequoyah." He wasn't sure what to expect—whether they would be dressed in Native American apparel or casual attire—so he was a little surprised when three men, all in suits and ties, acknowledged and headed toward him. They easily could have been mistaken for Wall Street executives.

"*Osiyo!*" greeted Harland. Wick had coached him on the Cherokee word for "hello." The three chiefs smiled with appreciation for being welcomed in their native tongue and likewise addressed their driver with an enthusiastic "osiyo!" and a handshake.

Representing the three tribes of the Tribal Council of the Cherokee Nation were Moss Settler, Cherokee Nation; Jack Horton, United Keetoowah Band of Cherokee Indians; and Joe B. Rowe, Eastern Band of Cherokee Indians. After collecting their luggage, Harland led the trio to a curbside location where he would return with the van for the hour-and-a-half drive to Rome.

Tsula Catawnee, the Cherokee shaman that Wick had located in western North Carolina, would be driving down from the Smoky Mountains late that afternoon, about a four-hour drive.

When the chiefs and shaman arrived, they were escorted to their rooms in the Watters's family cabins to refresh, after which they met in the large dining room to get acquainted over dinner and discuss details of the ceremonial walk-through the next morning at ten. The dinner table included heaping amounts of barbequed pork, southern fried chicken, fresh tomatoes, corn, squash, fried okra, and of course Uncle Tom's Famous Brunswick Stew.

As the discussion went around the table, the chiefs' overview of Cherokee heritage was enlightening and inspiring as the Watters clan continued to grieve the loss of their Uncle Tom.

After everyone had finished their meal, Moss Settler stood and spoke on behalf of all Cherokee tribes.

"Our three tribes make up the Tribal Council of the Cherokee Nation. Its representative body are citizens of the Cherokee Nation, elected to serve staggered terms. Tahlequah, Oklahoma, is recognized as our capital, with fourteen counties comprising our reservation.

"Our flag, approved by the council on October 9, 1978, is an orange field with the Great Seal of the Cherokee Nation at its center. The seal is surrounded by seven yellow stars with seven points, each of the stars representing the seven clans." Settler held up a flag while describing its symbolism.

"Colors are important too. Red signifies success and victory. White stands for peace and happiness. Blue means defeat and trouble. Black denotes death.

"Cherokees refer to ourselves as *Aniyvwiya,* 'the real people.' It is pronounced ah-nee-yah-*wee*-uh.

"Traditions evolve around music, storytelling, dance, foodways (our food is sweetened with honey and maple syrup), carving, basketmaking, headwork, pottery, blowgun-making, and flint-knapping.

"Except for tourists, Cherokee men do not wear big headdresses. Most of the Plains Indians wore them. Cherokee warriors would shave or pluck their heads except for a single scalp lock toward the back of the head. They would use it to tie one eagle or turkey feather to their heads.

"In the early eighteenth century, Cherokee men wore cotton trade shirts, loincloths, leggings, front-seam moccasins, finger-woven or beaded belts, multiple pierced earrings around the rim of the ear, and a blanket over one shoulder.

"As a rule, Cherokee men wore woven turbans made of hide or cloth. Calico, made of cotton and block-printed, offered a variety of designs. The cloth was attractive, cheap, and durable. Early turbans were worn bandanna style and tied around the head. Later, northeastern and southeastern tribes, including Seminoles, placed their own variation on this theme. Cherokee men adapted rapidly to white dress but differentiated themselves with calico turbans wrapped around the head, as Sequoyah was often seen. Leaders and prominent warriors decorated their turbans with silver bands or feathered plumes.

"As Cherokee people successfully adopted the customs, ways, and religion of their white neighbors, many Cherokees in general became prosperous merchants, traders, planters, teachers, writers, and tribal statesmen. Over time, the old customs faded, so the wearing of turbans, scalp locks, and feathers slowly disappeared.

"Cedar is most sacred to us. The wood from the tree, because it is so sacred, was used to carry the honored dead in ancient days.

"I hope I have adequately summarized our history, progress, and traditions for all of you. We welcome you to our capital at any time and thank you for your hospitality and good food tonight. Most of all, we genuinely appreciate your desire to honor the deceased, and us, in assuring Cherokee burial ritual and tradition are followed," concluded Settler as he took his seat.

Wick then stood up from the table. "Chief Settler, Chief Horton, Chief Rowe, and Shaman Catawnee, thank you all for being here, taking time to break bread together and come together as Americans. For Hollie and me, and everyone here tonight and tomorrow, we thank you from the bottom of our hearts for your wisdom and direction in preparing us for Uncle Tom's burial.

"Hollie and I have embraced the honor and privilege of organizing Uncle Tom's funeral. Everyone at this table—the Cherokee Nation and the Watters family—have made it possible for Uncle Tom to have the esteemed leaders of his heritage present, ensuring the rituals, traditions, and symbolism of this sacred service are respected for this man of great character, whose love for his Cherokee wife Aiyana and country were everlasting.

"Jennings Funeral Home has done an outstanding job, with your direction, in preparing the body. We'll have a driver ready to take all four of you over to Jennings at eight in the morning to ensure all protocol has been followed. They arranged for a Carolina cedar wood casket, and it is beautiful in its simplicity.

"Hattie will have a full breakfast waiting for you at this table by seven fifteen in the morning.

"The Watters party will be ready by the river at ten o'clock for your instructions as we walk through our respective roles.

"We wish you all a good night's rest and pray for your spiritual leadership tomorrow."

With that, everyone dispersed, Wick and Hollie making their way back to Papa Reed and Mama Rose's original cabin as the Oostanaula offered up its familiar and peaceful night sounds.

Lying wide awake, Wick checked his wristwatch. Five o' clock and he couldn't sleep anymore. He eased out of bed so as not to wake Hollie. He had a lot on his mind this morning, and a hot cup of coffee would help. Caffeine was king, his loyal catalyst.

He strolled out on the deck with the steaming cup and stood against the front rail as a light fog lingered slightly above the river. He sensed that the Oost current would be carrying memories as it flowed along its banks today. The river had always been a good friend to Wick, and he knew it would be an even better one for Uncle Tom now. While his body would be laid to rest beside it today, the river would forever carry his spirit. That was reassuring to Wick, knowing he could return here anytime to connect with the tall Cherokee.

He finished his coffee and returned to the kitchen, where Hollie had been at the sink watching out the window.

"Can I make you some breakfast, dear? It's going to be a long day," she offered, knowing well it would be for them both.

"Thanks, baby. I think I'll just have a bowl of cereal and a plate of fruit. My stomach is a little uneasy this morning."

Hollie decided she would have the same thing. Her stomach wasn't nervy right then, but it would be.

When the chiefs and shaman returned from the funeral home, they confirmed Jennings had indeed followed protocol. They had witnessed and participated as the body was washed and scented with lavender oil, the ritual allowing the herbal's strong spiritual properties to cleanse impurities. Then the body was wrapped in a white cotton sheet and placed in the coffin. The chiefs did not reveal it to Wick and Hollie, but all mourners would be surprised when the casket was opened during the service.

Shaman Catawnee went through the rituals with everyone involved in the service. Wick and Hollie would be seated on the platform with the three chiefs, the casket positioned directly in front of the shaman. Shaman Catawnee noted he would be speaking Cherokee throughout the service, except for the opening and closing prayers. Those would be delivered in English. This was to respect the wishes of Uncle Tom in staying as true to Cherokee protocol as possible.

The family had decided to set up one hundred chairs for the service. The burial would be around the platform and up the river bank toward Uncle Tom's cabin about fifty feet. A grave was freshly dug and the plot surrounded by an eighteen-inch-high, stacked-stoned circular wall with an open entry point. The family would later add a bench outside the wall, facing the river. Eight strong men provided by Jennings would carry the casket *on their shoulders,* led by the shaman, behind him the three chiefs, and then Wick and Hollie. The remainder of the Watters family would follow. Other mourners were welcome too.

On the ride over to the funeral home, the shaman noted that the chiefs had requested their driver stop where the three rivers met downtown so they might draw a vial of water each from the Etowah, Oostanaula, and Coosa.

Everyone was then dismissed to go back to their cabins, homes, or hotel to dress for the two o'clock services.

Wick and Hollie arrived back at the farm and funeral site a little early. All the chairs were set and aligned perfectly. The weather couldn't have been better: blue skies with a stray cloud or two, and the temperature around seventy-five degrees. In a matter of minutes, the guests began to arrive and take their seats. Ten minutes before the services, there was standing room only. Uncle Burton instructed the valets to drive their passenger and utility carts back to the dining hall to grab as many extra chairs as possible. The overflow attendance was indicative of the impact Uncle Tom had made on the community at large.

With everyone seated (just a handful standing now), the

black hearse followed closely by a limousine drove up slowly. The eight pallbearers, who looked like weight lifters, appeared from a black Suburban to the right. They methodically pulled the casket out, steadied it, then hoisted it on their broad shoulders. At that moment, the three chiefs emerged.

All three principal chiefs stepped out of the car in full Cherokee regalia. They were impressive in their native dress and reverent in their posture and approach to the platform. While white dominated the three chiefs' attire, each had an array of colorful adornments that distinguished their tribe from the other. Their most distinguishing feature: All were wearing multicolored turbans of calico, each distinctly different.

It was an emotionally moving, awe-inspiring moment for those in attendance. Everyone stood as the casket and procession passed by. Once the casket was seated in the bier, the shaman and chiefs opened the cap lid. Everyone was then invited to come forward to view the deceased while ushers kept the line moving.

Uncle Tom was also handsomely adorned with a turban, its red with modest green and gold designs printed over a silver stripe, reminiscent of the one worn by Sequoyah, the celebrated polymath and educator for whom he was named. His hands were placed together and holding an eagle's feather, venerating the sacred bird.

Above on the platform, the shaman began the service with a prayer.

"Pray that your heart, mind, soul, and spirit will not forget to look upward this day, to the One who is so much greater than we are. Turn downward and touch our Mother, the earth. Pray that everything you do this day will be in honor and reverence of our Mother Earth. Turn inward, place your hand on your heart, and pray that all you do this day will be true to the Spirit of God, the Spirit of Christ, the Holy Spirit who dwells within you."

At that point the shaman began to speak in Cherokee. Though his words were not translated, it didn't matter. They were reassuring, affirming that Uncle Tom's heritage was being honored. The shaman's animated words and inflections uniquely conjured up images of the deceased Cherokee, his character and integrity.

Shaman Catawnee then surprised everyone by playing an eloquent and moving rendition of "Amazing Grace" on his Native American flute. When finished, he and the three chiefs walked down to the casket, the shaman reciting the classic Cherokee prayer before closing the beautiful cedar coffin.

"May the warm winds of heaven blow softly upon your house. May the Great Spirit bless all who enter there. May your moccasins make happy tracks in many snows, and may the rainbow always touch your shoulder."

All in silence, the eight pallbearers hoisted the casket to their shoulders, following the shaman, the chiefs, Wick, and Hollie to the grave site. The Watters family and many of the remaining mourners would join.

Once there, the funeral personnel lowered Uncle Tom into his grave. The three chiefs followed, separately, sprinkling the water from the Etowah, Oostanaula, and Coosa inside and around the stack-stoned wall. The shaman ended the graveside ceremony with a Native American lament on his flute.

As the throng of mourners made it back to their cars, Wick and Hollie led the shaman and chiefs down to the dock, where Uncle Burton had secured two harnessed life jackets on a rope tied to the pilings.

Wick and Hollie, still teary-eyed, waited for the shaman and chiefs to reach the dock.

The couple looked one another in the eye. "Are you ready for this, Hollie?"

"As ready as I'll ever be, Wick."

From above, the shaman instructed them to walk out into the river together, holding hands if they preferred.

The two maneuvered out to about five feet of water, then stopped, facing one another.

"Now immerse one at a time, orienting and alternating to the east and then to the west seven times."

Wick went first, turning to the east and submerging, then back up and repeating to the west for the prescribed seven times. It was chilling, yes, but he could handle it. Now could Hollie?

She plunged under, then back up, repeating the protocol seven times also. She was visibly shaking by the end, appealing with her eyes to Wick, *I'm ready to get out now!* Quickly he pulled her next to him and up, out of the water onto the bank. Uncle Burton was waiting with warm blankets and towels, the shaman with fresh, new, and comfortable Cherokee clothing made just for them.

Once they were sufficiently warm, he presented each with a piece of tobacco and strands of sanctified beads. The tobacco was given to "enlighten their eyes" so they could bravely face the future, and the sanctified beads to "comfort their hearts."

The shaman and chiefs headed to Uncle Tom's cabin where they would sprinkle brewed tea throughout the house to ritually cleanse, while Wick and Hollie headed to their cabin. After lighting a warm fire, they watched as the tobacco smoked on a piece of burning cedar. They then settled on the deck with a glass of wine and much reflection, wearing their new Cherokee clothes and sanctified beads.

It had been a long four days, but they were at peace now . . . and Uncle Tom spiritually content.

"All that you can take with you is that which you have given away."
—from *It's a Wonderful Life*

Chapter Twenty

Frequent Flyer

Wick's travels for W.R.J. MacCallan Publishing would take him to all forty-eight contiguous states. About the time he would retire, Alaska and Hawaii would be included in the national footprint. Wick would let the next man or woman up navigate those distinctly different states for cover and profile stories. It certainly wasn't that they didn't have leaders worthy of an interview, *American Leader* just had not actively pursued or cultivated circulation in either state.

His forty-seven years crisscrossing America would find Wick in some unique venues, all memorable for different reasons.

As soon as Wick checked into the old Barbizon Hotel in Manhattan on Wednesday, July 13, 1977, he made it to his room on the sixteenth floor, shed his sport coat, loosened his necktie, and picked up the phone to call Hollie. It was about nine thirty p.m., and he was anxious to check on their four-month-old daughter, Marie.

"I finally made it, Hollie. It's hot as Hades here. Guess all this concrete holds in the heat. How's our little Marie doing?"

"Just fine. She's certainly had a good appetite today."

"And Joseph?"

"He's just fine, enjoying his new role as big brother."

"Glad he wants to help with his little sister. You can use it, I'm sure, even if he's only five. A little double teaming is a good thing. Please give them both a squeeze from Dad."

"Of course. Are you excited about your interview at the Downtown Athletic Club tomorrow?"

"You bet I am. My appointment with Mr. Cobleigh is about a twenty-minute cab ride. I'll allow thirty minutes at least. You never know when—"

Suddenly, at 9:36 p.m., the phone went dead, as well as all the power in the hotel, the Upper East Side, and all of Manhattan.

The Barbizon, built in 1927, famously became a women's hotel only, though in 1977 there certainly were plenty of men in the hotel when Wick checked in. They must have made special arrangements with the Downtown Athletic Club. Historically, the hotel didn't allow men above the ground floor until 1981.

The room began to get warm now that the air-conditioning was out. Wick went to the windows and discovered they weren't fixed. Each had a handle that enabled them to be rolled out.

On the street below, car headlights were the only source of light. The hotel was located one block off Park Avenue and only three blocks from Central Park. An eerie darkness settled over the world-famous park. No one could have known the blackout would prevail for twenty-five hours.

After an hour in the dark room, Wick decided it would be counterintuitive to remain. What if someone was smoking in their room and dropped a cigarette or an electrical spark caused a fire? It was a long way down from the sixteenth floor. He turned to plan B.

Wick opened his door slightly and could hear voices from the stairwell, which was almost directly across the hall. He took a chance, moved out into the hall, and felt his way square with the exit door, which he eased open. There appeared to be a family coming down, the man holding a lighted match.

"Do you mind if I follow you down?"

"*Non, merci de nous rejoindre,*" the man answered, which Wick interpreted as, "No, please join us." Though he certainly wasn't fluent, little did Wick know he would have to call on his college French this day to feel his way down sixteen flights of stairs in a pitch-black stairwell in New York City.

When they reached the lobby, several lighted candles had been positioned around the room, with pitchers of water and paper cups staged on a long table. The lady at the front desk had no encouragement to offer him as far as when the power might come back. They did confirm a severe lightning storm had hit the power plants that served New York City and all of Manhattan.

Wick thanked the French couple and their two children for letting him follow them down the stairs.

He then went out for some fresh air. No pay phones were operational, of course, so Wick couldn't call Hollie with the news but knew when she turned on the TV, she would learn the details.

In the meantime, Wick strolled down the sidewalk, listening to the night sounds up and down Lexington Avenue and East Sixty-Third, all the way over to Avenue of the Americas, or Sixth Avenue as New Yorkers preferred to call it.

Car horns were honking, loud music playing, police whistles

blowing, and blue and red lights flashing for several blocks. A number of sidewalk cafés and delis were unloading their food and beverages before lack of refrigeration spoiled it all.

While standing in a queue, Wick struck up a conversation with a fellow from southern California. He was in town calling on advertising agencies for his food trade magazine. As they talked, looting had begun farther up the street, hoodlums taking advantage of the darkness to crash window fronts and steal from defenseless retailers.

The Californian—Bob Slappy—and Wick decided on a deli sub and split a six-pack of slightly chilled Lowenbrau. They talked for a couple hours as humanity strolled by them. Some had dressed for Broadway, some for the summer heat, and some were barely dressed at all.

Both men had appointments the following morning, but each doubted whether those appointments would stand. The word on the street, from police and power workers at least, was that it could take another eighteen to twenty-four hours before power was restored. That meant the airport would be down as well.

Bob and Wick exchanged phone numbers and agreed to call the other whenever in Los Angeles or Atlanta.

When he returned to the lobby of the Barbizon, Wick saw what looked like a triage in a war zone. The floor was covered with sleeping bags and blankets in neat rows with two large tables of bottled water and snacks to either side of the room. Several people were already lying on the makeshift pallets, candles still the main source of light. A few flashlights kept by the hotel for emergencies like this were for personnel use only.

Wick whispered to the man now behind the registration desk that he was headed up to his room on the sixteenth floor to

THE SEASONS OF WICK'S CONTENT

retrieve his cleaning & soaking solution and storage case for his contact lens.

"Sorry, sir. For safety and security reasons, no one is allowed beyond the lobby," the bespectacled man whispered back.

"I understand, but I really need these items. I promise I'll go straight up the stairs to my room, grab them, and come straight back," Wick pleaded.

"I'm very sorry, sir," the man said, now slightly raising his voice, "but fire marshals have notified all hotels that absolutely no one can reenter their rooms."

Wick obliged with a nod and stepped back. He walked around the perimeter of the room in the dim light and then stopped on the other side when he came to what appeared to be an alcove. He leaned in and squinted over the apparent counter. There was just enough light to see a small reflection off the upper back wall, which showed a few rows of keys.

This must be the bellman's desk.

Wick quietly tiptoed around a row of sleeping guests to the nearest water table, poured about two fingers of water in two glasses, forced a full bottle in his sports coat pocket, and returned to his temporary habitat.

The swing door to the alcove was locked. He placed the two glasses and bottle at the end of the counter, then removed his coat. The top of the counter was low enough for Wick to swing one leg over then push up on both hands to allow the other leg to clear. Once in, he instinctively pinched out each contact and dropped it in its glass of water. He placed both on the floor in the corner, then rolled up his coat to pillow his head. It was literally lights out for Wick.

His eyes opened to the slight ray of sunshine that was bending through the two large lobby doors. He could see enough to gather himself and peek over the counter to find scores of guests still sleeping. Swinging himself back over the counter, he grabbed his coat and two glasses and stepped out onto a bright sidewalk. It took a few minutes for Wick's sensitive eyes to adjust.

The pair of backup glasses in my suitcase on the sixteenth floor sure came in handy.

He started up the street, sticking his head into doors until he found one that appeared to have access to a public restroom, allowing him to wash his hands, rinse, and reinsert his contacts. He was lucky, given the circumstances. He had spent a night on the ground in the city that never sleeps.

He used the downtime to make his way over to the Downtown Athletic Club. The plaque fixed at the entrance confirmed its founding and existence. A neatly typed notice on the official DAC letterhead declared "CLOSED. All meetings cancelled until further notice. The Board apologizes for any inconvenience."

Wick had missed his opportunity to visit the historic venue and take in all of the trappings associated with the vaulted Heisman Trophy. Ironically, by December of the same year—1977—the DAC board would approve women for membership in the elite club. It was a milestone decision for women, with all applicants as well resumed as the men.

In three hours, the power was back on at the Barbizon, and guests were permitted to return to their rooms.

Wick took a quick shower, dressed in some clean clothes, then risked taking the elevator down to the lobby. After checking out, he carried his luggage to the curb where a bellman blew his whistle for a cab.

"Where ya headed, sir?"

"JFK airport, assuming they haven't cancelled all their flights to Atlanta."

The bellman smiled, then opened the door as Wick tipped him a few dollars.

"By the way, thanks for allowing me to sleep in your space last night."

His smile wrinkled into an expression of bemusement as the taxi pulled away from the curb.

Franklin Felton was working on his dream of learning how to fly. He had banked enough hours with his instructor to qualify for his first cross-country flight in the month of April 1981. As the president and CEO of W.R.J. MacCallan Publishing, his family and management team were more than a little concerned that their key man was placing himself, and the company, in a vulnerable spot whenever he took to the skies.

Felton had no fear, however. When a student at UGA, he had run track for the legendary Forrest Grady "Spec" Towns, a member of the 1936 USA Olympic team competing in Berlin as Germany's führer, Adolph Hitler, watched. Towns won the gold medal in the 110-meter hurdles, while teammate Jesse Owens scored four gold medals in track and field, essentially dismissing the dictator and his boasts of Aryan supremacy.

Coincidentally, Wick had garnered two key interviews for *American Leader* in Dallas, Texas: Jack Evans, chairman and CEO of the Cullum Companies, a popular grocery executive who had been elected mayor of the city; and Jimmy Dean, most famous as a country music singer, TV show host, and entertainer, who had demonstrated remarkable business leadership in turning around a sausage brand that carried his name.

"Instead of buying a commercial ticket for your interviews in Dallas, why don't you fly with us," Felton suggested to Wick. "My flight instructor will be at my side the entire way."

Wick hesitated for a few seconds, knowing full well: *Hollie's not going to be comfortable with this.*

"As long as I can sit in first class," he joked, not having seen the plane yet.

It was a single-engine Piper, with no radar. The flight would be navigated visually.

At takeoff and throughout the trip, which included landing in Meridian, Mississippi, for refueling, the ride and skies were exceptional, the plane weaving around cotton-like clouds as they dissected the mostly blue sky enroute to Dallas's Love Field.

Wick, with not much wiggle room in his small space, was seated on the right side of the plane directly behind Archie, the flight instructor, and Felton was strapped into the pilot's chair. Archie appeared surprisingly young for an instructor. At just twenty-three, the young man was like a pudgy intern running coffee at the office, and Felton in his bomber jacket and aviator shades like Chuck Yeager preparing to break the sound barrier.

After Felton negotiated a smooth landing at Love Field, Wick picked up his rental car and was off for his midmorning interview with Jack Evans, then across town for his sit-down with Jimmy Dean.

Felton had a couple meetings with legacy advertisers. Archie had a bite to eat, then found an easy chair in the pilot's lounge for a good book and a nap. He and Wick would later be glad he did.

"There are three kinds of people: fits, misfits, and counterfeits," said Jack Evans in his interview. "Fits are the people who fit right in with their responsibilities; misfits are those who can adjust and change if given the right opportunity; and the counterfeits, you deal them out."

"I used to hate to come into this office. Icicles were hanging off of every door," remembered Jimmy Dean. "Everybody was scared to death. Nobody talked to each other.

"Everybody spent so much time covering their own ass that they couldn't get the job done. And people say, 'Since you took over this company, why this big turnaround? What have you done?'

"I permitted some damn brilliant people to do what they were able to do. Is that a big deal? Hell no. There's nothing to it. Realize a man's capabilities and say, 'All right, you can do it. I believe in you, go do it. And they do!"

Wick's interviews went well but longer than anticipated. Felton and Archie were ready to go, with the latter taking the pilot's seat since they would be flying at night for the last half of the trip back to Atlanta.

All went smoothly, but Wick's eyelids began to get heavy as the darkness crept into the cabin. Felton carried a thermos of caffeine, but one couldn't drink much knowing this wasn't a Delta flight with restrooms only steps away.

As darkness set in, Archie began to monitor weather conditions periodically in given locales. Halfway through north Alabama, the tower at Birmingham-Shuttlesworth International identified a thunderstorm headed southeasterly toward Atlanta. Archie radioed in asking for calculations on predictable wind velocity and vectors.

The Birmingham tower indicated no concern at that time relative to the Piper's coordinates.

About thirty minutes later, the radio picked up the tower at Hartsfield International in Atlanta. Calculations had been revised. Archie reported his air speed. The tower's calculus indicated the Piper would be able to land at Peachtree-Dekalb six to eight minutes ahead of the storm—a narrow window, but Archie appeared confident they would be fine.

Evidently Mother Nature disagreed. About five minutes in, the wind began to pick up dramatically as turbulence bounced and jerked the plane about. Suddenly, the plane's landing lights were fully reflected into the cabin. Archie suggested that Felton and Wick tighten their seat belts.

They had clearly run head-on into the storm clouds. Archie began to test the edges then pull back on the throttle as the wind shear punched and tossed the plane like a toy. He repeatedly tried to find an opening, but the shear would swing the plane up and then drop it down. He would immediately pull back and try another angle. With every setback, the engine momentarily stalled, triggering the air speed alarm as an amber light flashed unnervingly.

My God, we're not going to make it.

Wick literally began to pray.

Archie's face was stoic. His eyes focused on the instrument panel as the plane's lights continued reflecting off the imposing clouds.

After what seemed like an hour, though really about ten minutes, Archie circumvented the vertical shear and landed the Piper safely at Peachtree-DeKalb airport in northeast Atlanta.

When the plane came to a stop, its three occupants exited slowly. They had been tossed and turned so much in the frantic cabin, their shirts were rendered wrinkled and untucked. Wick's heart was still in his chest, but barely.

Felton somehow thought he could mitigate the frightening experience. "Wick, I know that was a little scary, but I just want you to understand we were never in any real danger."

Wick didn't respond. Instead, he glanced over at Archie, whose stoic face was now dripping with perspiration. He was about to give the young man a thankful hug. Felton? He wanted to punch him in the nose but thought better.

Wick Watters was abundantly more than content. God had indeed answered his prayer.

Hollie, Dad, Mom, and Uncle Tom are never going to know about this.

Wick was looking forward to his interview with Jack Brown in southern California on Monday, October 2, 1995. The chairman, president, and CEO of the Stater Bros. supermarket chain in Colton was an icon in the industry. He was savvy and adept at engaging the media. Jack made Wick feel like *he* was the VIP.

They met in the conference room, a separate table against the mahogany wall filled with orange and cranberry juices, pastries, apples, oranges, and hot coffee and tea. Knowing Wick was from the south, Jack made sure the offering included a box of Krispy Kreme donuts for his interviewer.

Stater Bros., with about 159 supermarkets, was the oldest and largest privately held supermarket company in southern California, and the biggest employer in San Bernardino County, the state's largest.

It was Wick's first visit to southern California, so Brown, who would be *American Leader*'s cover story for the November issue, broke the ice for the newcomer who had noted its exceptional weather.

"We have four seasons in California—earthquakes, fires, floods, and riots," asserted Brown, amending the universal parody slightly.

Brown, a veteran of the United States Navy, was unequivocally patriotic, as one of Jack's staffers in the communications and graphics department later confirmed.

"If you want Jack to approve something, just make sure it's in red, white, and blue."

Years later, when the Pentagon was under attack in Washington, DC, Jack noticed that none of the photos or illustrations of the terrorist attack included the Department of Defense headquarters. He challenged his graphic artist to come up with a poster that would integrate the visuals of that catastrophic day. He did, and Jack sent one to a friend working in the Pentagon who had survived the attack.

The friend tacked it to his office door. The next day, the friend called Jack to ask if he could send several more. Virtually everyone passing his office had poked their heads in the door to inquire where they could get one.

Jack got his VP of advertising on the phone, with instructions to print one thousand posters and expedite them to his contact at the Pentagon. Within two days, the FedEx delivery was distributed within the building.

Jack's contact couldn't believe the quick turnaround and how well his artist had captured the event. "The Pentagon is virtually wallpapered with your posters," the friend told him.

So, it was no surprise over the balance of his career that Jack Brown was honored with numerous special commendations. Three in particular stood out:

Semper Fidelis Award, from the Marine Corps Scholarship Foundation for his patriotic and distinguished service in support of the United States Marine Corps, presented by the Commandant of the Marine Corps.

The *Congressional Medal of Honor Society,* arguably the most elite organization of its kind in the nation, is comprised of only those Americans who have received the country's highest award for heroism under fire while risking their lives in action against US enemies. Jack was recognized for his years of contributions to the Society in promoting and perpetuating the principles upon which the United States was founded: courage, sacrifice, and selfless service.

A year later, during its Celebration of Freedom Gala at the Ronald Reagan Presidential Library, the Society would bestow the prestigious *Patriot Award.*

At the end of their interview, Jack Brown asked Wick to walk around to the side of his desk as he reached into his desk drawer. He then stood from his chair and pinned a full-color stars and stripes bar to Wick's lapel.

Appropriately, red, white, blue, and Brown were Wick's favorite colors of the day.

As Wick departed Colton for an appointment downtown at the *Los Angeles Times,* he wondered what the latest was in the O. J. Simpson murder trial. He turned on his rental car radio as he drove up the ramp to Riverside Freeway back to LA. After roving through classical, rock, pop, and country, he found an all-news station. The broadcaster confirmed that the jury foreman had notified Judge Lance Ito that a verdict had been reached. However, the judge had assured prosecuting and defense attorney teams he would allow at least four hours for everyone to arrive at the courthouse from multiple locations around the city. It was too late in the day for that allowance of time, so he delayed announcement of the verdict until the next morning, Tuesday.

Wick's penchant for being in a city or circumstance during a seminal event was real. Would that be the case while here in LA? It was three and a half years since the Rodney King trial when four LAPD officers had been tried and acquitted of beating Mr. King. For six days, opponents of the verdict rioted, with over 12,000 arrests and nearly 2,400 injuries as fires and looting pervaded Los Angeles County from April 29 to May 4, 1992. The verdict amid existing racial tensions brought the atmosphere to a boil.

Would that happen after the Simpson verdict was rendered?

After parking his car in the garage next door, Wick walked over to the art deco–designed *Los Angeles Times* building, now sixty years old, to call on Shelby Toffee, editor. When traveling, he would routinely call on the major newspaper in each city to gain insight and leads for the "Who's Who" in leadership around town.

Toffee accommodated Wick with a short list of half a dozen people, three men and three women, who had gained local press for their successes in SoCal, the abbreviated lingo for the region. After their conversation, Wick ask if Paul Chrisenberry was in, whom Wick had gotten to know when calling on the *Dallas Morning News* back in the '80s. He had left the Dallas paper to become the marketing director in LA.

"Hey, Paul. I have Wick Watters in my office. We're finished with our meeting. He wanted to know if he could come down to harass you a little." Toffee grinned, then laughed.

"Paul said only if you have a dozen Krispy Kremes with you."

Wick laughed out loud. *If only I had asked Jack. He would have let me take the box back to the room.*

He took the elevator down to the fourth floor and spotted the name plate on the office door. There sat Chrisenberry, whom Wick barely recognized. The man had really trimmed down. Obviously, he had dropped Krispy Kremes from his diet.

"You look great, Paul. Glad I forgot to bring any donuts this time." They sat down as Chrisenberry detailed how he was able to lose sixty pounds over the course of eighteen months, then Wick reviewed his meeting with Shelby and the excellent leads he had gotten. At that point, a colleague of Chrisenberry's, Charlie Lanier, stuck his head in the door.

"Oops, excuse me, Paul. Didn't know you had a meeting going on," he said, glancing over at Wick.

"No problem, Charlie. As a matter of fact, sit down and join us. This is Wick Watters from Georgia. He used to call on me when I was working at the *Dallas Morning News*."

The two shook hands, and then all three discussed the differences and similarities between Atlanta, Dallas, and Los Angeles. Charlie was an amiable fellow but seemed a little anxious as they spoke. During the exchange, Wick played off his meeting with Jack Brown earlier in the day.

"In my meeting with Jack, it appeared that the competitive landscape here in southern California is intense, which is a good thing for the consumer. You have such a variety of supermarkets to offer a diverse demographic." Paul and Charlie nodded their agreement.

Wick decided he would take his own straw poll between the two.

"Paul, you first. Y'all have Vons, Ralphs, Albertsons, Stater Bros., Trader Joe's, Sprouts Farmers Market, Whole Foods, Food 4 Less, Vallarta Supermarkets, Northgate Market, Smith's Food & Drug Center, Smart & Final, and many more.

"Where does your wife prefer to shop?"

"I would say Vons and Trader Joe's, and actually one you haven't mentioned—Bristol Farms."

"Interesting, Paul. That's a broad spectrum."

"How about your wife, Charlie?"

There was a poetic pause as Paul and Wick awaited Charlie's answer.

"Well, I'm divorced, and I don't give a damn where she shops."

He rose from his chair and quietly walked out the door.

Paul and Wick couldn't hold their breaths any longer. They both broke out laughing so hard that tears rolled out of their eyes. Surely Charlie Lanier couldn't hear them two floors above.

When the two finally collected themselves, Paul explained Charlie had just gone through a bitter divorce. His wife had left him after twenty-six years of marriage. The couple had no children.

When Wick returned to his room at the Double Tree at Los Angeles Street and West Second, he sat down and wrote Charlie Lanier a note of apology. Wick certainly had no idea what the man was going through, and genuinely regretted that an innocent conversation had inadvertently caused him pain.

When Wick woke the next morning, he hoped Tuesday's major event would cause no pain either. The LAPD had been placed on "modified tactical alert" the evening before, which potentially could be elevated to "major" in the wake of the verdict.

His hotel was just four blocks from the Stanley Mosk County Courthouse at 111 North Hill Street where the verdict would be announced. After making his round of phone calls, Wick dressed in his running clothes and shoes, then left the lobby to head in the direction of the courthouse. The streets all the way back to Grand Park, which was located across from the courthouse, were already lined with people carrying signs, mostly pro–O.J. Policemen mounted on horses were visible above the crowd.

Wick stood under the shade of a California oak as time passed. There was an audible, almost musical buzz throughout the crowd until silence fell upon everyone, especially those at the courthouse steps. One could sense that news of the verdict had seeped out of the building. When the actual words "not guilty" were dispersed among the throng, some people jumped up and down, waving their arms all around like the Lakers had just drained a three-point shot at the buzzer to win the NBA title; some quietly stood taller with their signs, and some were simply stunned.

The most important thing: no violence erupted. TV cameras and reporters moved through and around the crowd to record immediate reaction to the verdict. Opinions were articulated on both sides. The mounted police and their horses stood in place until people began to move out and back to their places to ponder the results of the last eight months plus.

Wick's return flight to Atlanta was uneventful. He caught a good nap while keeping his foot out of the aisle. The sky was a beautiful blue with a smattering of clouds. The airline food wasn't bad either. American Airlines was bringing Wick home from this West Coast trip, which couldn't have been smoother, including the landing and being on time at the gate.

Most all the aisle seat passengers were up on their feet, having retrieved their carry-ons from the overhead bins, and the middle and window seat occupants were waiting their turns.

A brief static filled the air as the speakers were switched on. "Ladies and gentlemen, this is your pilot. Please get up from your seats and exit this plane immediately. Don't delay or stop for your carry-on. Exit the plane now as instructed by your flight attendants."

Immediately everyone began to scramble. The attendants in the rear of the plane where Wick was seated were pointing everyone to follow one another up the aisle as quickly as possible. Wick overheard one of the attendants tell the other she had smelled smoke coming from the rear galley.

The aisle was moving, but not fast enough. The attendants blew the hatch on both sides of the plane at the emergency exit row windows. Wick had already pulled up his briefcase from under the seat in front when the plane landed.

One attendant then came on the speaker and told passengers everything was all right and to stay in the aisles to exit at the front of the plane. Some abided, but those in the rear weren't sure. The attendant nearest to Wick was sure she smelled smoke seeping in from the rear of the plane.

Some passengers chose to crawl through the now windowless openings. Wick was one of them.

The first two passengers in front of him made it through to stand on the wing and then back down a precarious stepladder that had been positioned as close to the wing as possible. The third passenger, an obese lady, wasn't as successful. Halfway out the opening, she got stuck.

Still expecting that a spark or fire in the fuselage could be imminent, Wick wasted no time. He put both hands on the woman's fanny and pushed hard. She rolled out onto the wing, then Wick threaded the portal like a needle. Once on the wing, he helped the lady step onto the ladder and take the first few steps down before one of the ground crew assisted her the rest of the way.

Wick made it down the ladder himself, but a woman on the plane's opposite wing lost her footing about halfway down and broke an ankle.

When Wick made it up the outside stairway to the gate, most of the passengers were holding back in the gate area for someone to explain what had happened. Two young men, waiting by the big glass window for their sister to exit the plane, both confirmed to Wick that flames had in fact been coming out of the plane's rear engine.

The pilot, now standing at the check-in counter holding a microphone, spoke to his passengers. "Ladies and gentlemen, as your pilot I want y'all to know we apologize for this emergency protocol and assure you that we were never in any danger."

Wick thought back to the Piper episode and Franklin Felton, but again he thought better.

San Antonio was always a favored destination for Wick, especially in the spring. Famous for the Alamo, its Hispanic culture, and Spanish Missions, San Antonio's Riverwalk meandering through downtown remains the city's most unique venue. Wick was told by a local executive that San Antonio's colorful Fiesta in April was the second most photographed event in America, behind the Albuquerque International Balloon Fiesta.

His interview on April 3, 1997, with H-E-B Grocery's Harvey Mabry, eventual president of retailing for the supermarket chain, was unique too. They met in the company's historic headquarters on South Flores Street where the old Arsenal stood. Dating back to 1859, the Arsenal had housed munitions for several wars. In 1985, H-E-B acquired ten acres of the complex and renovated the building for its corporate headquarters. The most dominant supermarket chain in Texas, H-E-B was also the largest privately held employer in the state.

How often did one have the opportunity to meet a man who rubbed shoulders with baseball royalty?

At just twelve years of age, Mabry and his Texas Little League team had their photo on the December 1951 cover of *Baseball Magazine* with Cy Young, the legendary hurler in whose name the holy grail of pitching is awarded for best American and National League pitcher.

Many young boys dream of growing up to be a big-league ballplayer. While they were dreaming, Harvey was hitting home runs in the World Series.

With H-E-B for thirty-seven years (he would retire after fifty years), the former Marine and University of Texas alumnus didn't pursue a baseball career, but for so many on that stellar Little League team from Austin, the groundwork had been laid for a promising business career.

"Having had success at an early age was inspirational for me, believing I could be successful doing a lot of other things as well, that I could do more than I was doing," said the former slugging first baseman.

"I was a hitter. An average fielder, but a pretty good hitter."

A young Cy Young would have been challenged by Mabry the day Texas played California. The winner would advance to the championship game. As it turned out, the fans at Williamsport saw Mabry hit not one, but two home runs.

Unfortunately, Mabry's bat and the team's good luck symbols didn't carry over against Connecticut the next day. All the Texas players had accumulated hat pins throughout the season, these becoming "good luck charms" as they progressed. Predictably, Harvey's pin bore the Marine Corps emblem.

Before the game began, Connecticut's coach told the umpire he would play under protest if the pins were not removed. He contended they were shiny and distracted his pitcher. Texas had to shed their pins.

"So, our luck ran out, but it was a great strategy. That coach knew exactly what to do," credited Mabry.

"He beat us before we ever got up to bat." The experience was a lesson in psychology and motivation for the future executive.

Calling himself an average store manager early in his career, Mabry admitted, "I was not doing a great job, and my aspirations were to hang on and maybe run a bigger store." Along came Ed Crane, then a vice president in the San Antonio division, who told Mabry he was district manager material.

"He really got me thinking about what I could do, rather than what I was doing. I found out later he told everyone that, but I thought he had singled me out because I was special. It really was the springboard for me."

"You can't really overestimate the potential that an individual has." Henceforth Mabry worked toward "unleashing that potential."

"We have a motto here that each and every person counts. That's really what I stand for."

Harvey Mabry was still hitting home runs, but the playing field was just a little different.

Delta flight 1044 departed Atlanta at 8:05 that Tuesday morning in 2001 for Washington-Dulles airport, Wick getting comfortable for a little early morning nap in seat 13-C after the pilot turned off the seat belt light. Being right-handed, he always preferred an aisle seat on the left side of the plane. That way he could avoid the dreaded middle seat and stretch out his right leg inside the aisle. On most flights the attendant would prompt him to remove it if he hadn't already by the time the beverage cart came through. Only on this flight they both forgot, but his big toe wouldn't. Wick took off his shoe to massage the aching digit through his sock, managing a smile for the sympathetic stewardess. He put his seat back and relaxed for a minute.

If this is the worst thing that happens on this trip, I'm a lucky man.

His nap cut short, Wick retrieved his briefcase from the overhead storage to review his interview questions for John Cabot, president and CEO of the Newspaper Association of America. Daily newspapers nationwide were being challenged more than ever as evolving technology and potential platforms questioned their relevance. Cabot's proactive leadership imagined a new paradigm for the industry.

Wick's appointment with the CEO wasn't until the next day at the NAA offices in Arlington, just outside the Beltway, but he would never make it.

He carried a cellular "flip phone," not one of the smartphones he noticed everyone begin using as the plane touched down at 9:43 a.m. An obvious concern showed on the faces of those riveted to their devices.

A wave of corroborating reports and descriptions rolled through the plane row by row. The intensity was palpable. By the time they reached Wick, the news became clear. America was under attack.

"One of the twin towers at the World Trade Center in New York has collapsed after a plane crashed into it," reported one of the passengers *(crash time, 8:46).*

"A plane hit the Pentagon too," said another *(crash time, 9:37, just six minutes before Wick's plane landed).*

By the time passengers were transferred to a tractor-like mobile carrier and shuttled to the arrival gate, the south tower had collapsed in New York *(crash time, 9:03).*

News hadn't come yet about a fourth plane, which went down in a field near Shanksville, Pennsylvania *(crash time, 10:03).*

Having no luggage checked, Wick proceeded to the rental car counter to pick up keys and then head to the hotel, a Holiday Inn near the airport. Not forty minutes after he had exited the plane, the entire airport was shut down. All concourses, gates, restaurants, bars, shops—everything had been emptied.

Once checked into his room, Wick immediately turned on the TV, called Hollie, then the office to confirm he had arrived and was safe in his hotel.

Oh gosh, I'd better call Dad and Mom to let them know too.

"Hi, Daddy. Just wanted you to know I'm in Washington and safe."

"Well, good. I'm glad to hear you had a good flight. How long are you there for?" asked Raleigh, with no hint of concern in his voice.

"Daddy, do you have the TV on?"

"Yes, I do. Watching the weather channel. Your mother is still in bed."

"You might want to change channels to one of the network or cable stations."

"Why's that?"

"Just change the channel and you'll see. There's been a terrorist attack."

When he did, Raleigh, and later Edith, became fixed like so many other Americans on the crisis at hand.

Wick contacted the NAA office, which had a recording confirming that the office was temporarily closed and all appointments had been cancelled until further notice. Wick was able to reach one of the NAA staff whom he had met before and happened to live near the hotel. He and Brady met at the Holiday Inn an hour later over coffee to discuss rescheduling the appointment with Cabot and, of course, the larger story continuously being updated by the broadcast media, especially in New York, Washington, and Pennsylvania.

All flights were otherwise cancelled and all planes grounded until intelligence agencies could assess the situation, including the potential for any further terrorist attacks on America. Save for frontline responders, hospital, emergency personnel, police, and military, the nation was paralyzed for a few days.

Wick's original return flight had been scheduled out of Norfolk on Friday morning, where he had another interview scheduled. That too was cancelled, but his chances of flying out of Norfolk were better than DC, and he already had a rental car.

If all flights were still grounded on Friday, he had the option of driving his rental car back to Atlanta. As one would expect, there was a run on rental cars everywhere. There would be countless stories of people driving rentals for several hundreds of miles, sharing rides to get back home.

 Wick was able to board his return flight from Norfolk on Friday. He would try to decompress, maybe take a nap, yet he felt guilty even thinking he could. So many innocent lives had been taken. So many families were left behind, grieving and hurting. The evil that had cast its long, dark shadow over America would have to be exorcised, along with the murderous malcontents responsible.

Chapter Twenty-One

Johnny Harris

"The holy passion of friendship is of so sweet and steady and loyal and enduring a nature that it will last through a whole lifetime, if not asked to lend money."
—Mark Twain, 1835–1910

Once in a lifetime a character comes along who fuels your adrenaline, feeds your spirit, and keeps your funny bone from rusting. A hefty guy with a big heart who loves a good laugh and the gifts he's been given. A new friend who brings depth and life-changing perspective, added dimension beyond work and family. An elixir of knee-slapping joy and stories aplenty to recount, whatever the season. It all renders a contentment unknown to the faint-hearted. Wick was fortunate to come to know such a character.

In early June 1987, his T-shirt soaked with sweat from mowing his lawn, Wick sat on his front porch steps watching the new guy fifty feet across the private drive digging away. A landscaping crew had just completed sodding his yard with several pallets of beautiful zoysia. Having used the tailgate of their truck to write a check for services rendered, he picked up his shovel and resumed his work.

Hollie stepped out on the porch to surprise Wick with a cold Coors Light.

"Thanks, baby. Say, Hollie, would you bring me one more please?"

She was puzzled until his eyes motioned toward the guy across the drive.

"Oh, of course." She nodded in agreement. Hollie went back inside to grab another drink.

All six-foot-three, 230 pounds of Johnny Harris powered through his size 12 Nikes, the right foot driving the spade shovel as it cut through the mound of mulch with a "swish" sound emblematic of the logo on his shoe. With such force, he reminded the Georgia red clay who was boss.

This big man with a husky physique and athletic frame was worthy of competition at any level. His attire certainly indicated he was ready for a workout. The ACA JOE's sweats were already absorbing the perspiration from his thirty-eight-year-old body, and the new white Georgia Southern ball cap bled moisture around the band.

The image struck Wick as amusing. Harris was standing in the middle of a dozen George Tabors, his favorite azaleas, all in plastic pots scattered around the pine island, waiting patiently for the man to dig them perfect holes. Augusta National couldn't have been more colorful, but Wick would soon discover that Harris could. His wit would entertain Wick as the two grew their friendship over the next decade.

Wick walked across the narrow drive running between their homes, clutching the two ice cold Coors Lights.

"Looks like you need a break," declared Wick as he extended

one of the cold brews to his new neighbor. "Welcome to the hood. I'm Wick Watters."

"Johnny Harris. Thank you. I do appreciate." They shook hands, then Harris popped open the Silver Bullet and took a long swallow.

"Your timing is impeccable. I was wondering when you were going to join the work party."

They laughed and shared their backgrounds while enjoying the refreshment. Then Wick grabbed one of the extra spades and they began digging in unison.

He would never forget his first neighborly encounter with John Crockett Harris, the big lug who loved azaleas.

The adventure had begun. This was the first of countless projects/work parties conceived by Harris.

Over the next ten years, Johnny would be farmer, landscaper, builder, barbecue chef, music man, big brother, and confidant. He could be a pain in the ass at times, yet would become the biggest-hearted, funniest friend Wick ever had.

It was the first of many trips Wick would make across narrow Ringling Drive, which ran deep into the woods of western Gwinnett County, about fifteen miles from downtown Atlanta. Blindfold anyone and they would swear they were in remote, rural country, not a few minutes away from one of the busiest interstate junctions in America. The neighborhood was generally calm and peaceful, with only six homes built on the twelve acres.

At least until Saturday morning. When Johnny got up and out, even the birds weren't ready.

Johnny and Wick became suburban sidekicks, much to the chagrin of their supportive and admiring wives. During the week, neckties and pinpoint, button-down oxfords were the dress of the day, but come the weekend the dress clothes were shed for sweat-stained baseball caps and branded T-shirts. The pair would lighten up Ringling while still being productive. Both lawns could vie for yard of the month in any neighborhood. Every Monday morning, a project was penciled in for Saturday.

If Wick were in the office, the receptionist would put the call through. If he were traveling, Johnny would have her run him down.

"Johnny, what's shakin'?" Wick would always begin. From there the conversation would diverge into planning the weekend's project.

"The pit, Wick, the pit."

"The pit?" Wick repeated.

"Yeah, we need to build a pit, to cook the pig we've been talking about forever."

"Where?"

"My backyard," answered Johnny.

"Oh yeah, that pit." Johnny's patio had become the "think tank" for most of their enterprises.

"How's your brick masonry, Wick?"

"Never laid one in my life, John."

"You're just the man I'm looking for, an able apprentice." Johnny laughed. "There's no way we can screw up."

Wick well knew, between the two, they could find at least a hundred different ways to screw up a project.

"How 'bout eight o'clock Saturday morning?"

"Johnny, you know we sleep in until nine on Saturdays."

"Not if I crank up the weed eater and blower by seven."

Of course, he wasn't kidding. Always up before the sun, he drank his perfunctory pot of black coffee and read the paper before raising the garage door for a rousing, gas-propelled "good morning" to the neighbors. Hollie, in spite of the nuisance, came to tolerate the big ox.

She had programmed herself to roll over and go back to sleep.

Johnny Harris was the best bond trader the Capital & Southern National Bank had ever seen, the entire city of Atlanta for that matter. Not since the 1950s had anyone from here or anywhere been able to deal with Wall Street with such a flair and acumen. In the financial world, his experience was tantamount to the experiment involving Eddie Murphy and Dan Aykroyd in the 1983 comedy film *Trading Places*. Wall Street partners and brothers, Randolph (Ralph Bellamy) and Mortimer (Don Ameche) bet on the cultural outcome of swapping the roles of commodities broker Louis Winthorpe III (Aykroyd) and poor street hustler Billy Ray Valentine (Murphy).

Johnny Harris, a history major from small-town Georgia with no experience in the cut-throat, high-pressure Wall Street world, a blockbuster bond trader? No way. Not a chance . . . but like Billy Ray, Johnny proved them all wrong.

Though he could care less about the limelight, Harris had become a southern star in the bond and mortgage banking galaxy, both for his mental acuity and knack for "living on the hedge." He had been written up in all the major trade journals, business pubs, and became the subject of a lengthy "Lifestyles" feature in the Sunday *Atlanta Journal Constitution,* complete with a handsome four-color photo in front of his and Wick's "pig pit."

If the pit could talk, it would regale with stories—sometimes real, sometimes embellished, but always entertaining. Whether they were sharing tales from school days or plotting their next work party, the "Ringling Brothers" never lost their grip. From the pig trip down to Milledgeville to pick up their first sacrifice for the new brick barbeque to the unauthorized removal of pines, Johnny and Wick did their best to cram one hundred pounds of adventure into a fifty-pound bag.

Their path to Ringling Drive had originated in different corners of the state, neither being among that shrinking elite who carried the unwritten title, "native Atlantan."

Johnny Harris had been born in Hinesville, about forty-five miles southwest of Savannah near the banks of the Notchahala river. Growing up there was no different than in any other small town across the South, though having a father who served three terms as mayor made Johnny's exploits in high school and college more public than his father and mother would have wished. All in all, Liberty County was better, certainly livelier, thanks to Johnny Harris and company.

Marshall Harris was more than just mayor of Hinesville. He owned the only downtown hotel, the local *Statesman* newspaper, the corner apothecary, more than six hundred acres of timberland, and knew most of the stories that gave Hinesville its color. He had returned from World War II and Normandy with a Purple Heart and one less arm.

Although Johnny was two years younger than brother Wes, he was more athletic, bigger, faster, and more savvy. Wes was shy but the better student, more dependable, and voted most likely to succeed by his classmates. Johnny was the most likely to get the two in trouble. Not bad trouble, though—mischief mostly.

While Marsh and wife Aza sometimes had their hands full with Johnny and Wes, raising two boys below the Gnat Line (an imaginary line from Columbus to Macon to Augusta) was really no more challenging than the annoying and tiny black fly. Increased rain in South Georgia would fill its rivers and render its sandy soil moist, creating a haven for larvae. The two sons, they could handle.

Their youngest was definitely the leader, though Johnny was never quite sure where he was going until he got there.

That first weekend, Johnny invited Wick over for a game of pool down in his rec room on Saturday night. Harris had all the shots: bank, break, breakout, call, carom, cut, jump, top spin, English—you name it. Wick wasn't a bad shot but not near as good as Johnny.

All the time Johnny was making his cue ball work magic, the stereo provided the background music that triggered enough adrenaline to make one believe he could make any shot because Roy Orbison, Booker T., Jackie Wilson, Sam Cooke, Aaron Neville, Etta James, James Taylor, Bobby Daren, Otis Redding, Dion, J.D. Souter, Major Lance, Brook Benton, Clarence Carter, Doris Troy, James Brown, Gladys Knight, Ricky Nelson, Ray Price, and Steve Miller said they could.

These artists and many more became the soundtrack for Johnny and Wick's projects and conversations, whether driving Harris's Chevy S-10 pickup over to Home Depot for garden supplies and equipment, or sitting in surf chairs on his raised patio accompanied by a brew or cocktail and the occasional fine cigar.

Finally, Johnny and Wick were on their way to Milledgeville.

Although the two embarked on the trip to pick up the aforementioned pig, the statement about Milledgeville, for anyone who lived in Georgia or was aware of its institutions, would draw a laugh. For many years Milledgeville was the location of the Central State Hospital, an asylum, and at one time the world's largest mental institution. So, there might be a few people around Ringling who would slap their knee and declare, "I told you so. I knew those two would wind up down there."

They were crazy all right, thought Wick. Why in the world did they have to drive nearly two hours to pick up a pig? *Surely there were pigs in metro Atlanta.*

"Yeah, but they're pets. You don't want to get arrested for kidnapping some little boy or girl's piggy, do you, Wick?"

Johnny's contact in Milledgeville ran a meat market and guaranteed him the best suckling around. For this inaugural barbeque, the pit deserved nothing but the best.

They left home at six o'clock that morning, and by 8:20 they were back on the road to Atlanta in the Pig Express. They had placed the pig on ice in a large commercial wash tub and covered it with a thick canvas. By the time they got back to Ringling, the temperature was in the low seventies and the oak wood had burned into some perfect coals. When Hollie came over, she and Johnny's wife, Mindy, came down to view the acquisition. The wives simply shook their heads.

"How can you cook that poor little pig with it looking right back at you, Johnny?" inquired Mindy. Hollie asked Wick the same question with her eyes.

"Ladies, you won't be worried about that tomorrow afternoon when you tempt your taste buds with this fire-roasted delicacy, rubbed with special herbs and sauces, especially when eaten with some Uncle Tom's Famous Brunswick Stew," Johnny explained, winking at Wick.

The women didn't offer any comments, just shook their heads again and returned home.

The Ringling Brothers were prepared for the all-nighter, moving their surf chairs down closer to the pit after restocking the wood. Overnight and into the morning's light, they treated the neighbors' noses to a tantalizing aroma that their palates were sure to envy.

All the while, the pig never blinked.

"You know, Wick, a split-rail fence across the front of your property and mine would dress things up a bit, don't you think?" quizzed Johnny late one Friday afternoon.

"Well, John, I'm always listening when your ideas for upgrading our property add value."

This was the next project that blossomed from the patio venue. It had been a pleasant spring day; the dogwoods were in bloom and many of the azaleas—George Tabor, Autumn Royalty, Bonfires, Ivory Evergreen, Red Ruffles, Pinks, Lavenders, Autumn Twist, Autumn Fire, Southern Charm, and Coral Bells—were on the verge.

Johnny was one step ahead. While Wick was traveling, he had measured and placed the order at the Depot. All they had to do was crank the truck and go get it, mostly likely in two trips.

"We better get a move on then. Hollie and I are grilling out at seven, and I promised we would go over to the mall for a late movie."

Johnny rose from his chair to fish the truck keys out of his pocket. "I'm ready to roll. If we leave now, we can make both loads within the hour and be ready to dig post holes early in the morning."

Wick walked over to give Hollie a heads up. Johnny had pulled the truck up to their mailbox, and off they went. Thanks to the store's efficient wrapping of the post and rails, they were able to make it in one trip. Wick was back in plenty of time to rub the steaks and get them on the grill. He and Hollie enjoyed their New York strips, baked sweet potato, and crispy asparagus with a glass of pinot noir, and still made it to the theater in time for the nine o'clock showing of *Dead Poets Society* with Robin Williams and Ethan Hawke.

At seven the next morning, the Watters were awakened by the sound of a chain saw.

"Oh my gosh, Wick, it's Saturday morning! What does that lug head think he's doing?"

"I'm sorry, Hollie. I know he's a pain in the butt, but remember we're going to set two split-rail fences today, and he's anxious to get started. You're going to love it when we finish."

"I better, or I'm going to finish him."

Wick gave her a kiss on the lips and promised he would remind Johnny what time zone they were in. Hollie smiled and slid back under the covers with a pillow over her head.

"Harris, is your clock set for daylight savings time, or did Mindy kick you out of bed?"

"Sorry, Wick. Did I wake your bride?"

"Of course you did. I would have been out here fifteen minutes ago if you hadn't."

"Well then, you should be thanking me." They both laughed but knew they would be in hot water if it happened the next Saturday morning.

By nine thirty the duo had marked all the spots where the rented auger would dig the post holes, broken for another cup of coffee, then begun to set the first of sixty posts. All the while, Johnny's boom box played the Four Tops, Temptations, and the Young Rascals.

When the job was done, Johnny and Wick invited the ladies to come view their work then sit down on the patio for a drink. It had been a labor of love, and Johnny was already planning their next project.

Johnny apologized to Hollie, of course. "Accepted." She smiled, knowing well that wouldn't be the last time he disturbed a sleep-in Saturday morning.

With only six houses on Ringling Drive, there wasn't much traffic. Except for the postman and an occasional delivery, the privacy was a luxury. Of course, with the Watters's kids, and Johnny and Mindy's two girls, birthday parties and car pools to baseball, soccer, softball, and church activities, the pace would spike at times. Over time, a couple potholes developed close to the Harris and Watters mailboxes.

"What's shakin', John?" Wick answered his phone on Monday morning.

"Wick, we've got to do something about those potholes. Eventually somebody's going to bust a tire if we don't. I called the county and they said because it's a private drive, it's not their responsibility. Let's grab the bull by the horns and fix it ourselves."

"How many bags of Quikrete do you think it will take?"

"Quikrete?" laughed Johnny. "Quikrete is a temporary fix. That asphalt has some age on it. We need to go with more solid concrete. I'll leave the Z car in the garage and take the S-10 to the office. At lunchtime I'll go over to Mingie Construction and get half a scoop of gravel, ample bags of cement mix, some sand, and tow the mixer home behind the truck. What time can you be out on Saturday morning? This may take awhile, plus we need to give it plenty of time to set up over the weekend before the workday begins on Monday. There should be enough room to set up a few cones to detour vehicles around the job for those who have to get in and out."

"I can be out there by seven, John. Just make sure you bring the boom box. Of course, we'll have to wait until nine o'clock to turn it up or Hollie won't be the only one on your case."

"Sounds like a plan, Wick. You might want to fill up our cooler with your Coors Light. I'll need some Bud Light if you don't mind."

"Got it, Johnny. See you Saturday morning."

Wick hoped they knew what they were doing or their heretofore pleasant and quiet neighbors would be teed off.

At 6:55 Saturday morning, Wick was at the "job site" ready to go. Johnny was finishing his coffee and cigarette.

"Punching in early to impress the foreman, Wick?"

"Of course, boss man. I've got a family to feed."

In no time they had the mixer churning. The motor wasn't too loud, thankfully, but did mean they would have to turn up the box when it was time for the work party concert. There was no traffic on the drive until about eight thirty. The veterinarian who lived in the next house down on Wick's side was open on Saturdays.

At exactly nine o'clock, Johnny popped in a cassette. The Young Rascals started things off with "It's a Beautiful Morning," his fanfare song. What a perfect entry to begin the workday, or any day. This was one of Hollie and Wick's favorites too, so if she did wake up, she would probably be smiling. Johnny always chimed in when Felix Cavaliere held the long note near the end of the song.

They worked until eleven when they stopped for a brew break. It was going to be near ninety degrees that day, which meant the concrete should set up faster. Of course, so would the Buds and Coors. Thankfully, Johnny had a few tall pines on the front edge, so they did have some shade until the sun moved over toward Wick's side.

About twelve thirty, Hollie brought out some finger sandwiches to sustain the guys. Mindy had taken the girls shopping. To their surprise, one of the neighbors on the far end stopped by the construction project, rolled down her window, and handed the guys a six-pack of Powerade, thanking them for taking the lead in getting the job done.

By midafternoon, a little hard work and a lot of Sam Cooke pulled them through, especially "Chain Gang."

The builder of both Wick's and Johnny's homes was their neighbor too. Fred Shilling's property was next to Wick's. He had a 5,400-square-foot house with a one-acre lake behind it and a tennis court on the right side of his home. The lake was stocked with fish and adorned with two lily white swans and one Australian black one. They were elegant in their paddles around the lake, but that's where any adoration ended. The white ones were tolerable, but the black one, renamed "Darth Vader" by Johnny and Wick, was noncongenial to say the least.

Beware any service technicians who came to service your home. If Darth spotted you, he came out of the water and up the hill at a fast trot. One time the air-conditioning tech wasn't aware that the black bird had crept up behind him. When the man turned around to grab a tool, Darth was staring him down.

The poor fellow turned white as a sheet and had nowhere to go. The determined black swan had the guy penned in between the brick wall and a compressor on one side and a needlepoint holly shrub on the other. The man's efforts to somehow spook Darth were in vain. He began yelling for help, for someone to come lure the swan away.

Luckily, Fred was home and came up to verbally scold the stubborn bird. He apologized to the serviceman, who was relieved and embarrassed at the same time.

Because Wick's house was nearest, Darth like to pick on him from time to time. One time Wick was rounding the corner of the garage, and there stood Darth. The black aggressor immediately flapped his big wings and chased after Wick, who somewhat nimbly jumped over the shrub in his path when he turned to run.

Johnny happened to be walking out to his mailbox at the time and saw it all. He was laughing so hard he was bent over. He never let Wick forget the episode, though Johnny too had his own confrontation with the swan.

The next time would be the last time for Wick. He was raking leaves in his backyard down near the lake. When he stopped at the next pile of leaves to catch his breath, he saw movement in the corner of his eye, and it was black. He turned and made eye contact with Darth, who now was stomping his way up the hill.

Wick waited patiently with his rake. It wasn't a blue-bladed lightsaber, but it was good enough. As the bird unfolded his big wings and craned his skinny neck, Wick swung the handle of the rake right under the white-banded red bill of the swan. Darth took a seat immediately, stunned. He wasn't the aggressor anymore. Almost on cue, the woozy black swan rose slowly, turned around, and waddled back to his lake asylum.

Wick hoped Fred had not seen the altercation. Shilling's swans cost about a thousand dollars each. The coast seemed to be clear. As for Johnny, where was the big lug?

Who's laughing now?

The guys' "bird watch" went from one breed to another.

The doorbell chimed three times on, yes, Saturday morning. Wick opened his eyes and looked at the clock. It was barely eight o'clock. *Oh no. What's he up to now?*

Surprisingly, Hollie wasn't awakened. Credit had to go to those new nighttime ear plugs she had just acquired. Wick pulled on his clothes and went to the door in his bare feet. When he opened it, the first thing he saw was a twelve-pack of Coors Light longnecks. Standing in the middle of the drive was Johnny, smiling from ear to ear.

To his right sat the S-10, idling with both doors open and the truck bed filled above the cab, so much it was a wonder the front wheels were still on the pavement.

"Looky what I got us, Wick!"

Having spent many a day on Papa and Mama Watters's farm, Wick recognized, rather *smelled* the heap after taking just one step out the door.

"What in the world are you going to do with all that chicken manure?"

"We're going to till it into the soil to superfertilize our tomato plants. Our Better Boys will be even Bigger Boys!"

Wick knew there was no use in debating this horticultural strategy. It was the afterburn that concerned him, and there was no way Hollie Watters would let him spread the acrid manure on their side of the drive.

"John, do you know how bad that stuff stinks, especially in hot weather? The neighbors, and that includes my Hollie, aren't going to be happy."

"It's rich all right, but our tomatoes are going to taste so good. The smell will go away in a couple days."

Wick knew better, and so did Johnny. They agreed one row of the tomato plants would be designated for the Watters.

It took about forty minutes for the two to shovel the manure into a 30- x 16-foot raised box of treated lumber. Then Johnny cranked the tiller, and the two took turns working the manure into the soil. By the time they had finished, their work pants and shoes may as well have been tilled in too. No way were they going into the washer. They hosed out the truck bed and rinsed off the tiller, then planted forty Better Boys.

After enjoying a cold brew on the patio, Wick returned home. He and Hollie were headed to the movies again, and Johnny wondered if maybe he had gone overboard with the chicken manure. He had seen the weather forecast for the next week. It showed highs approaching ninety degrees on Monday and throughout the week, unusual for mid-May and certainly not the seventy-nine degrees they had enjoyed on Saturday.

Come Monday morning, the Better Boy project had "matured." The pungent odor was so pervasive, Hollie literally sat up in bed.

"Wick Watters, I told you! That smell is oppressive! I'm not speaking to that big lug for a week!" And neither did the other neighbors.

Johnny and Wick had gone from Better Boys to "Bad Boys."

In June 1995, Johnny and Mindy were Bermuda bound on a surprise anniversary trip for the couple. Johnny had told her only what clothes she would need for the trip and that was it. He booked the flight and kept the tickets in his office desk drawer until the weekend of the trip.

Mindy had convinced herself it was either Sanibel, off the west coast of south Florida, or somewhere in the Keys. Mindy's parents would keep their twin girls, Andrea and Jacquelyn, for the week.

Johnny made her sit in the restaurant bar until he checked their baggage at the Delta counter. Only when they arrived at the gate did she learn their destination. She was ecstatic.

"Why you Johnny Harris! I am so surprised! I was convinced it was somewhere in Florida. This is going to be so exciting!"

"I think we'll enjoy it even more. Bermuda is famous for its pink-sand beaches; two popular ones are Elbow Beach and Horseshoe Bay. Jobson's Cove looks like a good place to swim. We're staying at Royal Palms Hotel, only four miles from Port Royal Golf Club. I knew that would be important to you." He grinned.

"Just remember, when you're golfing, I'm shopping." Mindy smiled back.

It was a great week for them both. They enjoyed a day in downtown Hamilton, the capital, visiting the interactive Dolphin Quest and dinner at the Barracuda Grill Seafood & Chops. The remainder of the week they laid on the beach, swam, snorkeled, and relaxed.

Johnny got in his rounds of golf, parring the tricky but majestic #16. Its green was set on the edge of a coastal cliff overlooking Bermuda's "electric blue" ocean. Meanwhile, Mindy made the most of his credit cards, and not at the Maritime Museum.

She reminded Johnny as he was leaving the room for his Friday morning tee time that she had made reservations for the dinner cruise that evening, embarking at eight o'clock sharp. "Don't forget to dress in your navy blazer and white pants. No khakis allowed."

He gave her a wink and thumbs up.

Finishing his round a little early, he returned to the hotel and decided to sit on the beach with a good book and a margarita, for which he kept the beach caddy busy. By the time Mindy arrived, the margaritas were ahead.

Mindy could read him like a book. That's why on her return she bypassed the room and walked straight out to the beach.

"You should have been there, Wick," he would later tell the story. "I looked up and squinted through the setting sun. All I could see was the silhouette of a woman holding two shopping bags in each hand, and she looked a lot like my wife."

Mindy set the shopping bags down evenly on the sand. Then she placed both hands on her hips.

"Johnny Harris, you're going on this cruise, whether you like it or not. You've got fifteen minutes to get up to the room and get dressed."

At that point, John spoke the two words all peace-loving men employ when in doubt, the ultimate and universal response in such dire circumstances.

"Yes ma'am."

It was a lovely cruise.

Chapter Twenty-Two

Playlist

Wick and Johnny's soundtrack for so many episodes of work and play looked like this:

"A Beautiful Morning," *The Rascals*
"A Girl Like You," *The Rascals*
"Ain't Too Proud to Beg," *The Temptations*
"Amen," Otis *Redding*
"Baby, I Love You," *Aretha Franklin*
"Back in the Saddle Again," *Gene Autry*
"Barefootin'," *Robert Parker*
"Beat It," *Michael Jackson*
"Bring It On Home to Me," *Sam Cooke*
"Candy Man," *Roy Orbison*
"Can't Do a Thing (to Stop Me)," *Chris Isaak*
"Chain Gang," *Sam Cooke*
"Changes in Latitudes, Changes in Attitudes," *Jimmy Buffett*
"Come Monday," *Jimmy Buffett*

THE SEASONS OF WICK'S CONTENT

"Cry to Me," *Solomon Burke*
"Dirty Laundry," *Eagles*
"Do What You Do," *Jermaine Jackson*
"Do You Believe in Magic," *The Lovin' Spoonful*
"Doggin' Around," *Jackie Wilson*
"Dream Lover," *Bobby Darin*
"Driver's Seat," *Sniff 'n' the Tears*
"Everybody's Talkin'," *Harry Nilsson*
"Falling into You," *Celine Dion*
"First Look," *Jimmy Buffett*
"For the Good Times," *Ray Price*
"For Your Precious Love," *Jerry Butler*
"Georgia on My Mind," *Ray Charles*
"Gimme Shelter," *Rolling Stones*
"Good Times," *Sam Cooke*
"Green Onions," *Booker T. & the MGs*
"Have I Told You Lately," *Van Morrison*
"He Don't Love You," *Jerry Butler*
"Honky Tonk (Part 1 & 2)," *Bill Doggett*
"How Sweet It Is," *Junior Walker & The All Stars*
"I Can't Help Myself," *Four Tops*
"I Got a Line on You," *Spirit*
"I Left My Heart in San Francisco," *Tony Bennett*
"I Say a Little Prayer," *Aretha Franklin*
"I Wanna Be Around," *Tony Bennett*
"I'm Your Puppet," *James & Bobby Purify*
"In the Midnight Hour," *Wilson Pickett*
"It's a Man's Man's Man's World," *James Brown*
"It's Up to You," *Ricky Nelson*
"It Was a Very Good Year," *Frank Sinatra*

"Just One Look," *Doris Troy*
"Lay Down Sally," *Eric Clapton*
"Layla," *Eric Clapton (unplugged)*
"Let's Get It On," *Marvin Gaye*
"Light My Fire," *José Feliciano*
"The Lonely Bull," *Herb Alpert & the Tijuana Brass*
"Lonely Teardrops," *Jackie Wilson*
"Love Man," *Otis Redding*
"Make It Easy on Yourself," *Jerry Butler*
"Margaritaville," *Jimmy Buffett*
"Mexico," *James Taylor*
"Midnight Rider," *Allman Brothers*
"Midnight Train to Georgia," *Gladys Knight & the Pips*
"The Monkey Time," *Major Lance*
"Moon River," *Henry Mancini*
"Moon River," *Jerry Butler*
"My Girl," *The Temptations*
"A Natural Woman," *Aretha Franklin*
"Oh! Darling," *The Beatles*
"Old Love," *Eric Clapton (unplugged)*
"Papa's Got a Brand New Bag," *James Brown*
"Rainy Night in Georgia," *Brook Benton*
"Ramblin' Gamblin' Man," *Bob Seger*
"Respect," *Aretha Franklin*
"Road Runner," *Junior Walker & The All Stars*
"Ruby Baby," *Dion and the Belmonts*
"San Francisco," *Scott McKenzie*
"Sexual Healing," *Marvin Gaye*
"She's a Woman," *The Beatles*
"Someone to Watch Over Me," *Linda Ronstadt*

"Something About You," *Four Tops*
"Start Me Up," *Rolling Stones*
"Statesboro Blues," *Allman Brothers*
"A Sunday Kind of Love," *Etta James*
"Tell It Like It Is," *Aaron Neville*
"That's Life," *Frank Sinatra*
"That's Why (I Love You So)," *Jackie Wilson*
"Think," *Aretha Franklin*
"Tipitina," *Henry Roeland Byrd*
"Tonight," *Kool & The Gang*
"Tracks of My Tears," *Linda Ronstadt*
"Travelin' Man," *Ricky Nelson*
"Try a Little Tenderness," *Otis Redding*
"Under the Boardwalk," *The Drifters*
"Up on the Roof," *James Taylor*
"Vincent," *Don McLean*
"Watermelon Man," *Mongo Santamaria*
"We May Never Pass This Way Again," *Seals & Crofts*
"What a Wonderful World," *Louis Armstrong*
"What's New," *Linda Ronstadt*
"Wonderful World," *Sam Cooke*
"You Can't Always Get What You Want," *Rolling Stones*
"You Don't Know Like I Know," *Sam & Dave*
"You Never Can Tell," *Chuck Berry*
"You're Only Lonely," *J. D. Souther*

Chapter Twenty-Three

Pamplona

Johnny and Wick had their favorite writers: David Baldacci, Pat Conroy, William Faulkner, John Grisham, Ernest Hemingway, Harper Lee, James Patterson, John Steinbeck, Thomas Wolfe, and of course Mark Twain.

Of them all, they were intrigued most with Hemingway's first novel, *The Sun Also Rises,* about a group of American and British expatriates living in Paris who travel to Pamplona for the San Fermin Festival to witness the running of the bulls.

They had discussed it numerous times, but never in front of the women. Hollie and Mindy would freak out if they knew Johnny and Wick were even considering it.

Running with the bulls. It was on their bucket list. Their wives would most likely laugh at first, then they would turn serious. Someone would say something like, "Well guys, sounds like a sure way to kick the bucket."

Of the tens of thousands who had run in the Encierro de Pamplona since records were kept from 1910, only thirteen men had been killed during the July event. Pretty good odds, but they didn't expect the ladies to buy that pitch. Actually, the running of the bulls had originated in 1591, but no odds would be good enough for Hollie and Mindy.

Was it all about being macho? Staring down death when it was headed your way like a freight train, or an adrenaline rush on steroids?

Whatever the rationale, it made no sense at all. They had children and one day grandchildren they would cuddle and spoil, read a bedtime story to, or take on a camping trip.

After much discussion, Johnny and Wick decided they would make the trek to Pamplona but were sworn to the sidelines for the running of the bulls, promising they would spectate only and participate vicariously through the runners. An estimated one million attended the seven-day festival, celebrating Saint Fermin, a holy man and martyr, revered as the co-patron saint of Navarre. On average, two thousand runners experienced the thrill of running with the bulls.

Hollie and Mindy even made them sign a notarized affidavit, pledging that under no circumstances would they cross the line, literally or figuratively.

The plane ride to Madrid was 4,325 miles, twelve hours direct. The guys flew first class, as Johnny always did, not because he was in the least pretentious. With his wide girth—muscle not fatty tissue (he took pride in lifting weights three times a week)—he couldn't fit in coach, especially when flying over 4,500 miles. By the time they landed in Madrid, local time was two a.m., and eight p.m. back in Atlanta. Boarding the train for the three-hour ride to Pamplona, Wick had made notes from his travel guide to look for the towns of San Sebastián, Donostia, Burgos, Logrono, Vitoria-Gasteiz, Alcalá De Henares, Haro, and Laguardia. Only problem was, it was dark the entire three hours. The sun rose just as the train pulled into Pamplona.

Johnny had been catching up on his sleep. Wick got his naps during the flight.

After the two checked into their room at the Gran Hotel La Perla, they took a quick shower then headed down for a bloody Mary at Hemingway's favorite haunt, Café Iruña, an art deco design founded in 1888 and just a minute walk across the Plaza del Castillo. The popular café/restaurant was featured prominently in *The Sun Also Rises*. Pamplona lured the acclaimed novelist nine times for the festival, running of the bulls, and bullfights. His first visit was in 1923 and most of the remaining '20s, his last two appearances in 1953 and 1959. He was very much a patron of La Perla on those visits too. Celebrities, the likes of filmmaker Orson Welles and English comic/silent film star Charlie Chaplin, also stayed at La Perla when in town.

A life-sized bronze statue of Hemingway leaning against the bar in Café Iruña encouraged photos, so Johnny and Wick obliged, their drinks hoisted for a toast. It was Saturday, July 5, and they needed to adjust their biological clocks to Spain time. Tomorrow they would find souvenirs for the wives and kids, and work in all the recommended restaurants and bars they could. One rocket blast would officially announce the beginning of San Fermin's festival at twelve noon on Sunday. The festival always ran July 6–14.

There were plenty of T-shirts promoting San Fermin and the

bulls, or *encierros,* for the children, and they couldn't resist buying their own matador hat, or *montera,* for the kids' next Halloween costume party.

If Uncle Tom were still alive, I'd get him one too!

Another must item was a don't-leave-your-hotel-room-without-it accessory: an authentic bota bag. Once you got boxed in by the tremendous crowd, the botas would come in handy, for both water and wine.

The concierge at La Perla directed them to a leather shop on the other side of the plaza. Sure enough, it was what they were looking for.

The traditional Spanish liquid receptacle, used mainly as a wineskin, was handmade from vintage Pamplona leather and sealed with pine resin. Each bota held one liter. Some bags were made with goatskin, but Johnny and Wick deferred to the leather.

They would compromise on the type of wine. Johnny was accustomed to a cabernet sauvignon, while Wick favored a pinot noir. They settled on a merlot. Having completed their shopping for everyone, they returned to the hotel to drop off their bags of souvenirs.

They hired an English-speaking local, Santiago, to walk them through the bull run route, posing first in front of the Monumento al Encierro. The monument depicted life-sized statues of the bull run in action—six bulls and two steer with ten runners in front.

"At exactly eight a.m. each morning, six ferocious fighting bulls are released from the Calle Santo Domingo corral," explained the Spaniard. "They are 'escorted' by six well-trained steers that herd the bulls and keep them on course. They weigh at least thirteen hundred pounds."

"That's a lot of bull," Johnny inserted. Santiago smiled and continued.

"About two hundred runners line the bull run route. Some sprint alongside and sometimes in front. The total distance is about half a mile, and normally takes less than four minutes."

"What a contrast," chimed in Wick, "when you consider the Kentucky Derby back home, a mile and a quarter track, takes a little over two minutes."

Santiago nodded in agreement.

"After two rockets are fired, the *mozos* [runners] begin sprinting along the narrow streets with the bulls chasing. At the end of the course, the bulls charge down the ramp of the Plaza de Toros, through a red door which leads them out to the bull ring and the corral in the back."

Following the bull run, somewhere between five o'clock and seven, spectators would fill the stadium to watch professional matadors fight the same six bulls that had run earlier that day.

Santiago noted that the bullfighting ring was used only during the festival. The rest of the year it is open for self-guided and tour-guided groups. Plaza de Toros was constructed in 1922 with a seating capacity of 13,000 and enlarged in 1967 to almost 20,000, making it the third largest bullfighting ring in the world, behind Madrid and Mexico City.

It was time to taste some serious tapas and any other Spanish delights in historic Old Town, where the narrow, curving lanes and classic cobblestone streets invited Wick and Johnny in.

They sampled three different tapas bars: Calle San Nicolas, Mandarra de la Ramos, and Bar Cerveceria La Estafeta. Their scientific research prepared them to make the right choices: Simply walk up to each bar and point to the ones that looked most appetizing. They then washed each meal down with a popular Spanish beer at each restaurant. First the Mahou Maestra, then the Estrella Galacia 1906, and finally, Ambar Export Tres Maltas.

They were well fed and ready for bed. Ready as they would ever be for Pamplona the next morning.

Wick had all kind of memories flooding through his mind that next day. Somehow, he never truly thought this trip would happen. He thought it was just talk, like guys do when they have a bottle or glass of inspiration in their hands.

Yet here they stood, in Pamplona, Spain, in great position right behind the wooden fence and before the Curva de Mercaderes. The bulls would have to slow here to make the turn, then pick up speed for the stretch down Estafeta.

The traditional two rockets were fired and the run was officially underway. As the mozos sprinted out, Johnny and Wick could hear the bulls in pursuit, snorting, stomping, and headed their way at the pleasure of thousands of anxious spectators.

As the bulls passed ayuntamiento (city hall), first Johnny, then Wick, noticed pushing and shoving going on behind them to the left. Evidently someone was upset their view was being blocked. A couple of young guys who had hoisted their girlfriends on their shoulders appeared to be the problem. Tempers heated quickly, then shoving turned into fighting. The next thing Wick saw was one of the girls, whose boyfriend had been punched and knocked backward, flipping off his shoulders and over the fencing.

The girl landed headfirst on the cobblestone street. Everyone seemed frozen in time and place.

Except Johnny Harris.

In what felt like a nanosecond, Johnny's big body swung over the wooden fence and on top of the girl. Johnny covered her as one of the bulls trampled him. One of the herding steers began to nudge the bull around and back on course, but not before one of his horns tore a twelve-inch gash in the back of Johnny's leg, which brought on profuse bleeding.

Now Wick swung over the fence, ripping off his shirt and applying it as a tourniquet.

"Hold on, Johnny, hold on! Medics are on their way. We're going to get you to the hospital," Wick pleaded into his ear, not at all sure Johnny was conscious.

Two ambulances pulled up. The girl, still unresponsive, was placed on a stretcher first and into one of the ambulances, which sped off.

Another medic quickly reinforced Wick's makeshift tourniquet with a medical one on Johnny's leg. Wick's biggest concern now: *Get us to the hospital before he bleeds out! H*e jumped into the ambulance and sat silently as the medic continued to monitor Johnny's vital signs. His heart rate was elevated, and his blood pressure was dangerously low. Wick had no idea of Johnny's blood type, but if it were O positive, he told the medic he was ready to transfuse if needed.

They arrived at Navarra Hospital's emergency entrance, and Johnny, still unresponsive, was rushed into surgery. Wick whispered into his ear again. "Hang on, Johnny. We're at the hospital and the doctors will take care of you now. I'll be here with you as long as it takes."

As they rolled Johnny back, Wick looked down and realized he was covered in blood and not wearing a shirt. One of the admitting nurses gave him a scrubs top to pull on. He asked if she knew how the young girl who had preceded Johnny into emergency was doing.

"Tests showed she suffered a moderate, but not severe, concussion. She's resting and will be held overnight for observation."

"That's good news, and my friend will be happy to hear. He saved her life."

She had heard over the news what had happened and agreed, assuring Wick she would give him an update on Johnny as soon as he was out of surgery.

Wick suddenly realized he needed to call Hollie and Mindy. They had planned to watch together on one of the cable channels. It was a little after three p.m. back home. He immediately found a quiet alcove down the hall. They would be frantic.

"Hollie and Mindy, I'm sorry I haven't called yet. I'm at the hospital. Johnny's still in surgery." Hollie had put her phone on speaker so they wouldn't have to repeat any of the details. "Were you able to see what happened on the TV?"

"Oh, they've played it back several times already. It was horrible to view. Mindy and I are so concerned. Was Johnny conscious when they took him in at the hospital, and how are you?"

Wick assured Hollie he was fine, just sick that he couldn't get to Johnny sooner. "No, he was not responsive when they took him back to surgery.

"Mindy, we're all praying for Johnny. He's my best friend, and I'm here all the way. Ladies, I'm so sorry yet so proud of Johnny. He sacrificed himself to save that girl's life. I believe in all my heart he's going to make it. He lost a lot of blood, but he's a healthy, physically fit guy and has the will to beat this."

Wick filled in all the details and how quickly everything went once they stopped the bleeding. He assured the ladies he would call back as soon as Johnny came out of surgery and he was briefed.

After he found a washroom to clean himself up, Wick sat down with a cup of coffee in the corner of the waiting room.

Two hours later the nurse tapped Wick on the shoulder. In spite of all the caffeine, he had nodded off.

"Mr. Watters, sir?" Wick sat up suddenly in the chair.

"Yes!"

"I hated to wake you. Please follow me. Dr. Sanchez would like to speak with you." Wick was so thankful that they spoke better English than he did Spanish.

When the nurse pushed the door open, there lay Johnny with his eyes closed. Dr. Sanchez stood by the bed.

"You're a good friend to Mr. Harris," he acknowledged. "If you hadn't applied your tourniquet when you did, we wouldn't be standing here right now."

"Thank you, Doctor Sanchez. I only wish I had acted sooner. For a big man, Johnny's pretty quick."

"You ain't seen nothing yet, Wick," piped in Johnny.

Wick froze, not believing his ears. Johnny had been unconscious and near death. Now he was slowly opening his eyes, although he couldn't keep them open. The lights were too bright at the moment.

"Johnny, how do you feel?"

"Like I've been run over by a bull."

The doctor, nurse, and Wick all smiled at one another. Well, *they* did. Wick almost lost it.

"Wick, how is the girl? Tell me she's okay."

"The nurse told me she's going to be fine. The young lady is resting now with pain and sleep medication, though understandably traumatized."

"You saved her life, Johnny. No doubt about it," punctuated Wick.

"That's great news, Wick, and thank you, Doctor, for keeping me above ground. I really like Pamplona, but I believe I'll watch your bulls on TV next year."

Doctor Sanchez laughed. "Yes, that would be my recommendation, Mr. Harris. You can still wear your bota too."

Then everyone joined in a good laugh with the doctor.

"I second that, Johnny. Our wives will make sure of it. I spoke to them a couple hours ago, and I'm about to step out and give them an update. All things considered, I believe they're holding up well."

"Thanks, Wick. Tell Mindy I love her and look forward to coming home to her and the girls. Give my love to Hollie too, and tell her that her husband saved my life. Also tell her I can't wait to get back in our yards and make some music." Wick couldn't help but laugh.

Doctor Sanchez jumped in to summarize. "Mr. Harris, we had a lot of intricate work to do in reattaching ligaments, muscle, tissue, and nerves while maintaining blood flow. Amazingly, there was no major damage to the artery nor any broken bones. It seems the bota bag still hanging around your waist somehow managed to be in the right place at the right time. You're going to have a handsome scar down the back of your leg, but given the circumstances, you're very fortunate. Two, maybe three more nights in the hospital, and you should be ready to get on a plane back home."

Johnny managed a smile and momentarily winked one eye. "Start packing, Wick."

On Friday morning, Johnny and Wick boarded their flight to Atlanta, with botas intact.

Johnny Harris would live fifteen more years to age sixty-three. After a successful run at investment banking, he and Mindy retired to Sanibel Island, where they and the girls walked the shell-filled beaches endlessly. He would be there for their high school and college graduations, walk both girls down the aisle on their wedding days, and read bedtime stories to three grandsons and one granddaughter. He died from heart failure on March 27, 2012, his life filled with many great memories. If he could do it all over again, he probably wouldn't change a thing.

Well, maybe. Surely, he would add another song or two to the soundtrack of contentment.

Chapter Twenty-Four

Sage

Marie, the Watters's daughter, came home one Saturday afternoon holding a cute tan-and-russet male puppy with mostly black ears and nose. She was smiling ear to ear, telling her mom she had found the dog while walking in Atlanta's Piedmont Park. She obviously wanted to keep the rescue, but Hollie headed her off at the pass.

"Young lady, we already have a house full of cats. We can't take on a dog now, not in the house. If we were spending more time out at the farm, maybe, but you'll just have to find someone else to take him in."

"Mom, can I at least keep him in my room overnight? It's getting a little late to start calling around. At least I'll have some time to think about who among my friends might be the best to raise him," pleaded Marie.

"You're asking a lot of that puppy, Marie. His first and last night in a strange place, and he's probably going to cry some too. If you're willing to get Otto's old kennel out of the garage and paper-proof the floor, we'll agree, but you absolutely have to find someone else."

Without hesitating, Marie headed straight to the garage with the pup. She was seventeen and becoming more like her father every day.

"Remember, Dad is traveling and will be home tomorrow night. That dog had better be gone by the time he arrives. He's already put his foot down about no more pets in the house, and you know it."

"Yes ma'am," acknowledged Marie, though inside she knew it was going to be difficult to let the pup go.

After she fed the puppy some of the late Otto's dried food, she cuddled with him in bed, scanning her brain for the best prospects among her schoolmates. Before placing him in the kennel she walked the dog, encouraging him to do his business. As he sniffed every plant and shrub within his new but temporary orbit, she suddenly had an idea.

"Joseph! He could rescue this sweet dog. He's in between school, living in a rental house, and could use the company." Marie couldn't wait to get back up to her room to phone her older brother with the good news. Meanwhile, the dog continued to explore and sniff.

There happened to be a supermoon that night, which meant the moon was full and at its closest point to earth. As a result, its illumination was 20 percent brighter. As the moonlight caught the curious puppy's eyes, Marie sensed this canine would be something special.

She had just learned the meaning of a new word in her English class: wide experience, great learning and wisdom. She would name him "Sage." After all, she was the one who had "found" him

Sage portrait (Wick's soulmate)

in the park. Marie would reveal to her mom months later that a lady standing in the park was giving the puppies away, hoping by offering the dogs to passersby that enough people would take them in to keep an animal shelter from euthanizing them.

"Joseph, I've got a big surprise for you. You're just going to love it. As a matter of fact, I wish I could keep it, but mom won't allow. There's just no room for it."

"Is it a new car?" he joked.

"You wish. It's even better. It's a new puppy I rescued in Piedmont Park."

"Come on, Marie. Get serious. I don't have room or time for a dog. I'm working five, sometimes six days a week. Plus, I don't have a roommate anymore, and I'm considering going back to college next semester."

"Exactly why you need Sage."

"Who's Sage?"

"Your new dog. I gave him that special name."

"He's not my dog."

"You've got to see him, Joseph. He's so cute, and so smart. His eyes talk to you. Please don't turn him down, Joseph. He's perfect for you, and you for him. Please let me bring him over tonight."

"Well . . . ," her brother hesitated. "Can you bring him over now? I'm working the evening shift today." Joseph was tending bar at Elwood's Tavern in Decatur, an Atlanta suburb.

"YES! I can have him there within the hour. Oh, thank you, Joseph, thank you so much. You won't regret it. I promise."

"Mah-reeee," he drew out her name. "I haven't said yes yet."

Deep down, she knew he would.

When Marie pulled into the driveway of the little house, Sage began barking. As soon as she opened the car door to snap on his leash, he dodged her and was running toward the front door where Joseph was standing with folded arms. They weren't for long, though.

Sage made a leap from the bottom step, up three more, and stood on his short hind legs extending his front paws as far up Joseph's leg as possible.

"Calm down now, Sage. You're just a hyper little boy," said Joseph as he tried to subdue the energetic pup. Once pulled up into Joseph's arms, Sage stopped trembling and gazed up at the new guy. Their eyes connected, and then Sage licked Joseph on his cheek. The two were bonding, like long-lost friends.

Marie's stomach went from churning to a blissful calm. She walked up the steps and wrapped her arms around her brother and Sage, holding on tight.

This match was meant to be.

Sage's love, loyalty, wisdom, charm, and enthusiasm would be unending.

Joseph and Sage would log a lot of miles over seven years. Their stay in Decatur lasted barely a year. Then an opportunity came along for him in Colorado. A group of twenty-somethings were taking their turns at a revolving door in Denver. The city was primed for the younger demographic, traveling from all parts of the country to see what the gateway to the Rocky Mountains was all about. Eight to ten guys from Atlanta, depending on the number of job openings, were sharing an apartment and rental house near Cherry Creek Reservoir while employed at a couple of landscaping companies in the metro area. Some might be there for as little as six months, others a couple years. Joseph fell into the latter category.

Joseph was restless at the time. He hadn't been ready to jump right into college after graduating high school, so it was no surprise one Saturday afternoon when he made the announcement.

"Dad, I'm moving to Colorado," he said, trying to be as efficient with his words as possible.

"For how long, son?"

"Not sure, maybe a year or so."

"Do you have a job lined up?"

"Yes. A friend of mine from school is coming back to Atlanta, and I'm going to take his place at Brickman's."

"You've already discussed this with your mom?"

"Yes, sir. She's fine with it." Wick figured Joseph was playing one against the other, but that was all right. His son was nineteen and certainly capable of making his own decisions. Whether they would be the right ones, only time would tell.

"What are you going to do with Sage?"

"He's going with me, of course."

His best answer yet.

With Sage at his side, Joseph would be safer, Wick believed. The dog was Joseph's guardian angel, no doubt, and it wasn't like Joseph couldn't hold his own. He had wrestled in a state championship program.

"So, when are you and Sage hitting the road?"

"Tomorrow morning."

"Are you going to do all the driving?" Joseph appeared puzzled at first, then broke into laughter when his dad could no longer keep a straight face.

They hugged, and Wick handed him a C-note for gas.

Wick thought back to the first time he'd met Sage at the house in Decatur. He was just a year-old "puppy" then. The dog had stood up on his back legs and placed his front paws on Wick's shoulders. The veterinarian later told Joseph the dog was likely part border collie and German shepherd, maybe a tad Belgian Tervuren, too.

To Wick, he was all that and more.

Joseph spent two years in Colorado, during that time skiing and snowboarding seemingly every resort in the state. Then an opportunity surfaced in Oregon. A grower in McMinnville called with an opening in sales. The commission structure was appealing, so Joseph and Sage (aka the Lewis & Clark expedition as Wick liked to refer to them now) struck out for Oregon.

"It was just me, Sage, and Mother Teresa," Joseph said, referring to himself, the dog, and his shotgun. They overnighted in a sleeping bag under a clear but cold Montana sky at a state line national park.

After two and a half years, Joseph was transferred back to Colorado where he would be in management training for several months. But he had one problem. He wouldn't be able to keep Sage. The apartment the company had secured for him during his training program did not allow pets.

Joseph was faced with a tough decision. His network of friends in Denver had mostly departed, so there was no one on whom he could rely with confidence to keep Sage until he was finished with his training. That idea was a stretch anyway.

A couple lady vets who had treated Sage in Oregon confirmed they had a client with a large farm who said he would be glad to take Sage. He had other dogs he could run and play with.

Joseph took a deep breath. "Tell Mr. Gallagher I'll get back with him tomorrow."

Joseph knew Sage would have a good home. He also knew, with the training program grooming him to take over a nursery somewhere in the Southeast, he likely would never see Sage again. He called Hollie and Wick that night to discuss his dilemma.

"Do y'all have any ideas before I give Sage to the farmer out here?"

Wick and Hollie read one another's eyes immediately, then began gesturing with their hands, waving them toward their chests in unison.

"Yes, we do, son. Tell the farmer you really appreciate the offer, but you've found a couple in Atlanta that's going to take him."

Joseph nearly dropped the phone. "Are you serious, Mom and Dad?"

"We've always viewed Sage as your rock. We're not about to let him get away from you now, after seven years by your side. We're keeping him in the family."

"Actually, there's an interview I need to do in Denver. I'll book a flight for early next week. When I'm finished, we'll put the big boy on a plane back home."

"Done deal, Dad. Thank you both so much!"

Because of the warm weather in June and the protocol for flying larger animals in the cargo hold, Sage's flight times were limited. The dog would have to take a night flight, which would arrive nearly five hours before Wick's. Marie would be there to pick up the canine. Joseph would remain in Colorado for his training program. On June 9, 2006, Sage would be on a Delta jet to Atlanta.

Joseph and Wick drove Sage to the airport at midnight, working through the paper protocol with the cargo agent while selecting a kennel sufficiently large for him to inhabit during the four-hour flight. A water bowl was attached to the kennel door, but no food was allowed.

Saying goodbye to Sage, who began whimpering as they turned to walk back to the car, was like leaving your three-year-old at day care for the first time. His whimper became a bark the farther they walked. The plane was a wide-body 747, so with the kennel stored in the belly of the plane, it would definitely be loud.

Marie was early at Delta cargo to receive Sage. She was concerned. *Will he still remember me?*

As soon as the desk agent at the airport's cargo depot announced the flight had landed, she positioned herself straight across from the bay where all kennels were delivered.

She could recognize the whimper. When the kennel appeared, Sage's head was craning, looking for someone, anyone he might identify.

"Hey, Sage! How are you, boy? Remember me?" Sage definitely recognized her voice. As soon as the agent opened the kennel, Sage broke out running toward Marie and lunged forward, his big body nearly knocking her off her feet. She hugged and petted him as he jumped around for joy.

As soon as the attendant helped load the kennel in her SUV, they were on the road home. Marie called Joseph before she got onto the interstate to confirm she had his precious cargo in tow.

She heard a big sigh of relief in Denver. Wick and Joseph swore then they would never ask Sage to board an airplane again.

Several months later, his management training completed and now headed to South Georgia to run the nursery in Cairo (pronounced "K-row," like the syrup), Joseph asked his father if he could pick up Sage on the drive down.

"No sir," answered Wick politely. "I'm not letting him go. I just can't, son. Your mom and I have really become attached to the big boy." Joseph smiled. He had known the answer before he asked the question, and knew that his parents would ensure Sage got the best medical care possible as he advanced in age—and be pampered and spoiled along the way.

For the next seven years, Wick and Sage became soulmates. Hollie gave him excellent care and attention when Wick was traveling, but the two became inseparable when together. Every time Wick ran errands around town, Sage rode in the back of his 1987 Jeep Cherokee, affectionately known as the "Sagewagon."

Sage slept on a life raft–size bed beside Wick and Hollie. When Wick rose every morning for coffee, Sage would raise his head. Wick would whisper down to the dog, "You go back to sleep now, buddy." They enjoyed their favorite routes when out on Saturday mornings, swinging by the places where Sage would hang out the side window, matching barks with his local buddies as they chased alongside the Jeep.

All you had to do was ask, "Do you want to go for a ride?" The next thing you saw was Sage's rear end bouncing down the stairs to beat Wick to the door. Hollie and Wick finally had to develop a code to signal their intentions. Even spelling out "R-I-D-E" would trigger Sage's euphoria. The dog could actually spell.

Every Saturday night, Hollie would shape a pound and a half of ground sirloin, which Wick would grill and Sage would devour. As the big boy grew older and his weight was of more concern, they switched Sage to one pound of grilled ground turkey. He devoured it just as fast as the sirloin.

On July 26, 2011, Sage would make his first visit to the UGA Veterinarian Hospital, the first of many. Over the next two years, he would bounce back every time, in great part because of the excellent, special care he was receiving, but in no small part because of his determination to live.

Surgeries from cataract to cancer, removal of a mass on his left shoulder, "old dog disease" episodes of no movement in his limbs, nose bleeds from high blood pressure, diabetes, and more—he endured it all.

Counting all his medications, including sticking him periodically with the glucose meter, Wick and Hollie tended to Sage twenty-five times a day. They were fully committed to keeping the dog as healthy as possible.

It seemed a miracle every time his handler, way at the other end of the hospital hall, would yet again walk Sage back to the Watters, anxiously awaiting at their end. The staff always smiled as brave Sage made his way down the long hall to return home once again.

Until August 14, 2013. On this day the doctor at UGA shook his head, signaling the dreaded "no" to Wick. It was time, past time, to put Sage down.

On Sage's last night, Hollie and Wick slept with the dog between them. They wanted him close till the very end.

Sage's regular vet would come to the house the next morning to free Sage from all pain. It was a bittersweet moment. So many memories washed over Wick and Hollie as they tried to hold together during the dreaded but inevitable process.

The most memorable . . .

Hollie held Sage by his collar until Wick's car came to a stop in the drive, then released him when the car door opened. Wick bent down to hug the dog around the neck. Sage always sensed when Wick was on the way home, detecting the sound of the car's engine as Wick approached the driveway. No matter what kind of day at the office or road trip he had experienced, Wick was always boosted by Sage's rush to welcome him home.

At 11:28 a.m. on Wednesday, August 21, 2013, Sage's stilled eyes said goodbye as the canine's primary veterinarian put him down in the Watters's home. Wick and Hollie laid their hands over his heart until the last beat. Wick gazed deeply into Sage's brown eyes, then whispered into his ear that he had been a godsend, indeed a blessing that Marie and Joseph had rescued, nurtured, and passed on to them.

Arrangements had been made with a pet crematory in Decatur to pick up the body. They followed the special white truck, its red taillights flashing the entire thirty miles in a pouring rain. When they reached the Decatur city limits, the sun had pierced the dreary gray canopy of clouds, creating a beautiful and prophetic rainbow arced overhead.

Hollie was numb. Wick was sobbing.

He remembered what Uncle Tom had once told him . . . "Never be ashamed nor apologize for a tender heart. It's just as important as a brave one."

Chapter Twenty-Five

Still Watters

Edith

One of young Wick's favorite images of his mother was her dancing barefoot, literally, in the kitchen. Edith loved music, and when a popular song came up on the old AM radio, she turned up the volume. So, it was no surprise that when the disc jockey played "Barefootin'" by Robert Parker, she was ready to roll.

"Sunbeam" as her classmates at McHenry High had nicknamed Miss Beamish, had perfect rhythm. Every step, up and back, was in sync and on the beat. Edith made the most of her five-foot-four-inch frame.

As she danced from the side screen door over to the back one in the kitchen, she was laughing and enjoying every moment. Wick was outside on the carport in a rocking chair watching, likewise rocking and rolling with the beat.

Their three-year-old German shepherd, Blackie, began howling from the back steps where he had been using the screen to scratch his back.

"Listen to him sing," smiled Edith when Raleigh entered the kitchen.

"Edith, he's not singing, dear," he said above the din of the music. "He's crying, wailing like a siren because it hurts his ears!"

Blackie would finally move on and leave the stage for Sunbeam.

When out of school during the summer, Edith and older brother Leonard would stay up late downstairs listening to the vintage RCA radio playing boogie-woogie tunes as they rolled their cigarettes. It seemed everyone was smoking in those days. Advertising and the movies certainly romanced the habit. They had to keep the music turned down, however, for parents Julius and Emma were asleep upstairs.

Her go-to beverage was coffee. No matter if it were July and hot as a firecracker or January and cold as a glacier, Edith would prefer a cup of coffee. As she grew older and began to have episodes of migraine headaches, the caffeine proved helpful.

Her senior year at McHenry High, she was voted "Neatest," and she continued to hold that title the rest of her life. It was especially evident in her kitchen, in the clothes she wore and the laundry she folded. Whatever she was cooking or baking, everything had to be just right, from the presentation of the food on the plate to the taste of it all.

Thanksgiving and Christmas were special for sister Diane and for Wick. Out of school for the holiday season, the two would watch as Emma and Edith spread out all the ingredients for fruitcakes, as well as coconut, German chocolate, and red devil cakes; pecan, pumpkin, sweet potato, lemon ice box, key lime, chess, coconut cream, and apple pies; plus a large bowl of banana pudding. All the while Julius cracked pecans, walnuts, and Brazil nuts.

Gathering at the Beamish house in the summertime for

homemade ice cream was a family tradition too. The ladies would ready the recipe for the paddle can, and the men would crank at least two six-quart freezers. Vanilla, peach, and strawberry were the most popular flavors.

All these wonderful traditions began to phase out years later. Edith, at seventy-four, began showing signs of some form of dementia. Raleigh said she would read the newspaper, then twenty to thirty minutes later ask him if she had. Other signs, like remembering birthdays, anniversaries, and even what day of the week became challenging. Raleigh, Diane, and Wick huddled up and decided it was time to set an appointment with a neurologist.

They all waited in the anteroom for the technician to complete Edith's MRI (magnetic resonance imaging). Everyone was anxious as they each, in their own way, braced themselves for the results.

When the doctor came in with his file folder, he immediately sat down beside Edith on the examination table.

First, he asked her what day it was, who was the current US president, who was the previous one, in what county she lived, and what year she was born. She could not answer any of the questions correctly, though she did offer some guesses. She looked so pitiful, defeated, and embarrassed.

Wick dropped his head and stared down at his shoes.

Oh my God. This breaks my heart. My mother, for so long vibrant and full of life, is now reduced to such vulnerability.

The doctor studied his charts momentarily, then confirmed a diagnosis of Alzheimer's.

The family walked together to the car, stopped on the ride home for a bite of lunch, then took Edith Watters home, all wondering how long she would be able to stay.

When they got her inside, Wick excused himself to the bathroom at the end of the hall. There he closed the door tightly, grabbed a towel from the vanity cabinet, and buried his face in it to muffle the sound of his tears. *Damn this disease!*

Over a period of about eight months, the degenerative disease continued its assault on Edith's ability to navigate through her day. In the mornings she had more lucidity, but by the evenings she became more agitated and disconnected. New medications offered some hope of slowing down her degeneration, but it was just a matter of time before Edith would have to be admitted to an Alzheimer's-dedicated facility.

By late March of 2003, the family admitted her to a traditional nursing home that now had a dedicated Alzheimer's ward. She had her good moments when medicated, but for the rest of the time Edith did not know where she was.

Wick would bring her a chocolate Frosty on every visit. Sometimes she was up to walking to the end of the wing to sit on the glass-enclosed patio. Most of the time it was a sunny day and Wick could recount stories and mention old friends, which would elicit a smile.

After an hour or more, Wick would give his mother a hug and kiss before walking out of her room and down to the exit door, dreading the next time he would see her dazed eyes.

By mid-April 2004, her condition had worsened, exacerbated by the emphysema in her lungs. The nursing home doctor immediately had her moved to Rome's largest hospital. After two days in the ICU, Edith was admitted to a private room. Wick spent three nights with his mother, now unconscious. He left to drive back to his home outside of Atlanta, comforted that his sister, Diane, was already en route to the hospital.

Within an hour of arriving, his sister called. "Wick, I just left the hospital. Mother has taken a turn. Her breathing is more labored, and her hands so swollen. I whispered into her ear that I loved her, and her grandchildren and grandbabies all loved her too because . . . I don't think she's going to make it through the night." Diane was crying and hyperventilating. Wick told her to go home immediately and rest. He was getting in the car and headed back to the hospital. He didn't phone his father. Raleigh had spent all morning and most of the afternoon with Edith too, and Wick knew he was wasted. No need for him to come back now. Wick didn't want both of them in the hospital.

Wick made the two-hour trip in an hour and a half. He had his amber flashers on all the way. When he made it to the room, a nurse was checking his mother's vitals. Edith's breathing was more labored than when he'd left. The nurse didn't voice any specifics, but her body language said Edith's passing was imminent.

Wick pulled a chair close to Edith's bed. The wall clock showed 10:20 p.m. He settled in with his eyes trained on his mother's every breath. She would not die alone.

In what seemed like only a few moments later, the clock now read 1:08 a.m. Edith's breaths had become shallow and slower. Every downstroke of the ventilator seemed it could be her last. At 1:12 her breathing stopped, and so did Wick's world. He was holding his mother's awfully swollen hand. He told her, like he had so many times this lonely night, that he loved her. Forever. Now she would have no more pain.

The nurse hurried out to message the doctor, who would pronounce the death.

The ventilator was quieted now. The only sound was Edith's

pacemaker still delivering electrical pulses. Edith's heart was now stilled, and Wick's was broken again.

Edith Virginia Beamish Watters passed on April 22, 2004, at age seventy-six.

Raleigh

Viewing the annual Army–Navy game, arguably the most classic rivalry in all of football, was a must every December for Wick and his father. Because Raleigh had served in the US Navy from 1943 to 1946, it was extra special for the pair.

Woodrow Wilson was the first US president to switch sides at halftime (1913), ceremonially walking across midfield to show neutrality. It also established a great tradition in honoring all the young men and women who, after graduation from Annapolis and West Point, would serve their country faithfully as commissioned officers around the world.

When Wick took son Joseph to his first Army–Navy game in Philadelphia in 1999, the hundredth renewal of the classic, he was hopeful Raleigh could join the celebration. But Edith's health came first, of course, and circumstances just would not allow. However, Wick packed the frame of his father dressed in his navy uniform, and they proudly held it in a photo taken in the stadium with midshipmen marching in the background.

Wick and his father always pulled for the underdog in any game not featuring their team of allegiance. The two found themselves forming the same alliance in one of Raleigh's last stays in the hospital.

Diane's call to her brother came in before six o'clock on this weekday morning. She was at the hospital with their father. He was in intensive care, with one lung full of fluid and the other one in trouble "Doctor Starling has just given him an antibiotic with a name six syllables long. He says it's the absolute strongest he has, and he also asked me if Daddy has a living will. It's that bad, Wick."

"I'm getting dressed as we speak, sis. I'll be there as soon as I can," Wick promised, guessing he would be on the front edge of rush hour traffic if he left in ten minutes. He hopped on the interstate and settled in for another motor marathon, at somewhere around sprint speed.

Without any accidents to navigate around and, luckily, no flashing blue lights appearing in his rearview mirror, Wick made this trip in an hour and fifteen minutes. He grabbed his duffel bag and sprinted to the third floor and ICU. The nurse directed him to Unit 7 directly across the busy room.

Diane was sitting just inside the door, and Raleigh was either asleep or unconscious.

"He's hanging on," she whispered. "Doctor Starling said we should know if the antibiotic is kicking in effectively within the next hour." Just then, a nurse came in and asked them to step out. The nurse was going to insert a suction device into their father's right lung.

Levofloxacin was the amped-up antibiotic they were administering intravenously, another nurse told Wick.

It was painful to *hear* Raleigh's gasping and moaning when the tube was inserted, much less *feel* the apparatus down one's throat.

"Oh . . . oh . . . oh . . . OH!" he cried out. Wick and Diane cringed.

In about five more minutes the procedure was done.

"I know that must feel like torture to y'all, but we have to get as much phlegm and fluid out as we can with each procedure," explained the nurse. "We were able to get more out this time, and we always mitigate the pain with an effective sedative."

"How often will you do this?" asked Wick.

"The doctor has ordered them out at least every two hours."

Doctor Starling came by an hour later, noting that the antibiotic was beginning to work and the mass of bacteria was starting to shrink. "How your father's body responds in the next twenty-four hours will be critical," he punctuated. Wick could see Diane was worn out. Her day had begun at four a.m. with a call for an ambulance.

"Sis, I want you to go home and get some sleep. I'll let you know if anything changes. Don't worry now. Daddy is going to pull through this. He's a World War II vet. He's tough and will beat this back."

Diane was buffeted by his assessment and took him up on going home. After all, she was his big sister.

After grabbing a quick bite in the cafeteria downstairs, Wick settled into the reclining chair beside Raleigh's bed. He knew the nurses would be in and out all night, but that was okay. This wasn't his first rodeo in hospitals.

He was here to take his father home. He and Raleigh were used to being underdogs, and Wick was content with the role.

When he did nod off to sleep, Wick dreamed of his college graduation back on June 6, 1977. He didn't remember much about the speaker, other than he was the regional president of the Federal Reserve Bank in Atlanta. It was outdoors, in Sanford Stadium, and the full sun and attendant heat had been oppressive, especially in those black caps and gowns. It was worth it, though. He had his diploma in hand, and his mother and father there to bear witness.

He was worried how they would take the heat, though Edith was tan and wearing a beautiful floral sundress, and Raleigh was certainly used to the heat at the paper mill. He looked sharp in his sport coat and tie. Edith always coordinated his colors well. After University President Davidson dismissed the ceremony, Wick made his way down to the field to meet in the west corner of the stadium where former UGA mascots were memorialized. The white English bulldogs had been well pampered.

Raleigh and Edith were standing there, perspiring like everyone else around them. However, his father was crying. The only time he had ever seen that was when Papa Watters had passed. Edith gave Wick a kiss and offered her congratulations, then Raleigh stepped out. His arms fell around Wick like a yoke, and he squeezed his son like a vice. He then released his grip and stepped back. No words were necessary. Wick had redeemed himself and made his parents proud, the first in the family to graduate college.

Wick Watters could not have been more content.

Now back at the hospital in 2010, it was five thirty in the morning as the nurse pulled back the curtain to let a little light in. Wick sat up quickly to check Raleigh. His breathing seemed normal, and the nurses were ready to do another round with the suction device.

Wick stepped out, not fully awake, but a cup of coffee would take care of that.

The sounds emanating from the room were less offensive, and Raleigh wasn't moaning severely. The nurse finished and came out to tell Wick his father "was showing improvement." Dr. Starling would fill in the blanks when he made his morning rounds.

Three hours later, the doctor stepped in with his clipboard. "Mr. Watters, things are looking much better. We're going to add another bag of the Levofloxacin, and if we stay on track, you just might walk out of here in twenty-four to forty-eight hours."

"I'm all for it, Doc," managed Raleigh.

Wick and Diane rotated shifts the next twenty-four hours, she preferring the night shift because of her work schedule. When he arrived the next morning, Wick got a good report from the nurse, and Diane was feeling more confident too.

"Daddy should be coming down the home stretch today," Wick told his sister.

After she left, Wick assumed his post in the recliner.

"How are you this morning, Wick?" asked Raleigh with a surprisingly strong voice. Wick quickly stood up.

"Well, the important question is, 'How are you?'"

"I've been better."

"Are you hungry for some breakfast?"

"I sure am. Would love some eggs and toast, maybe some Cream of Wheat."

"Don't go anywhere. I'll check with the nurse."

She assured Wick that he could eat this morning, and breakfast would be served in the half hour.

By the time Wick returned to the room, Raleigh had gone back to sleep.

The report was stellar the next morning. Raleigh's oxygen level had returned to 96 percent and all vitals were holding steady. Raleigh's spirits were high, and his expectations were to check out of "this hotel" today.

"Let's see what Doctor Starling's assessment is this morning," smiled Wick.

While they waited, he thought about Edith and how much he missed her. Wick regretted there were things he wished he had told his mother, that she could appreciate before the Alzheimer's laid waste to her mind. That wasn't going to happen this time, whether his father walked out today or next week.

"Hey, Daddy."

"Yes, Wick."

"I want you to know that you've always been my hero."

There were about five seconds of silence.

"And you have always been mine."

Raleigh Watters was released from the hospital at one p.m. the next day, Diane's SUV waiting under the portico and Wick ready to help him onboard.

Fast-forward to January of 2011: Raleigh was eighty-six and had just returned from six weeks of physical rehab after breaking his kneecap on the concrete driveway. In his haste to get to the mailbox for the morning paper, he had tripped and tumbled to the ground, half of him on the drive, the other on the dew-filled grass. He lay there for a good half hour before the neighbor's Australian shepherd discovered him in the dark of the morning. The savvy dog stood over the man, barking back toward his house until Tony, the owner, came to the rescue.

Raleigh had been busy the previous four years, surviving two automobile accidents while totaling two small pickup trucks. One flipped over in the grassy median, leaving him hanging upside down in his seat belt until firemen could cut Raleigh out and pull him through the window. A big lunch at the Partridge Café and toasty warm truck cab had lured him to sleep. In the second accident a couple years later, he was on the receiving end of a T-bone. He sustained no serious injuries in either accident.

He survived prostate cancer, dating back to 1992, and lived with a pacemaker for ten years. When his heart began to "flutter" or beat irregularly, his cardiologist switched the pacer with a defibrillator, Raleigh's best friend for some four years.

In late January 2012, Raleigh was signed up for in-home hospice care, a program not available when Edith was battling Alzheimer's. Hospice care was originally created for terminally ill cancer patients only.

Once again, the gutsy sailor defied the odds. With his doctor's written recommendation, Raleigh qualified for a new hospice category, "Adult Failure to Thrive." Ironically, his heart issues did not make him a candidate for the cardiac category, since he had never had a heart attack, failure, valve issues, nor a stroke. He'd only had an episode of angina at age fifty-six, with future routine angioplasties showing no serious blockages.

He was comfortable in his home and had regular weekly visits from hospice nurses to assess medicines and check vitals. Later in his care cycle, as he became feebler, nurses would give regular baths.

His mind and wit remained sharp to the end. One time when Wick lost his temper over the "scroll" of a grocery shopping list the caretakers had left him, he said something stupid. Standing in the kitchen, he reminded himself that his father sitting in the den had heard every word he said.

You selfish fool. What do you have to complain about? Your fading father, World War veteran, child of the Depression, and your HERO doesn't need to hear your whining!

Wick walked around the kitchen breakfast bar and knelt down in front of Raleigh. "Daddy, I owe you an apology. You didn't need to hear that crap. I'm so sorry I lost my temper."

He looked up at Wick with a grin and a wink.

"I think you found it."

Then, in early November 2013, Wick was still celebrating the birth of his only grandson, Reed Watters III, on October 7. Joseph and Wick had wanted to show the now six-week-old boy to his great-grandfather, but Raleigh had been feverish and they didn't want to take the chance right now. In lieu, Joseph brought the newborn's cotton hat to prop on top of the chest across from Raleigh's bed so he could see it when he awakened every morning.

At the office, Wick had a call waiting on the line from Barbara, Raleigh's primary nurse. "Wick, I thought I should call this morning. Your father has been running a low-grade fever since last night. I've kept it down for the most part, but I'm concerned how much more he can sustain. I really think you should plan to come this afternoon or early evening. I'm sorry, but I don't believe he will make it through the night."

That's all Wick needed to hear. He made a quick call to update Hollie, grabbed his jacket, and was out the door. A packed overnight bag was in his car, as it had been for the last month.

When he pulled into the drive, two extra cars were there. *Oh no, am I too late?*

Nurse Barbara opened the door, and Wick saw his sister seated on the couch.

"Charlene is going to take care of your father tonight. I'll be leaving at six, but you have my cell if needed."

"So, who belongs to the other car?"

"That's Grace. She's back visiting with Mr. Watters. She's the hospice chaplain."

"Oh," said Wick. "I'll go back to say hello. How's Daddy?" *Thank God I'm not too late.*

"He's about the same. His fever has spiked a couple times, but we're okay right now."

When Wick saw his father, he thought the man seemed a little pale. "How you doing, Daddy?"

"I've been better."

"With all these pretty women here, you should be up dancing. Do they know you are used to *Dancing with the Stars* every week?"

That brought a smile to his face, and the chaplain's too.

They all visited for about thirty minutes; well, Raleigh listened. Grace was appropriately named. She was able to reach Raleigh through a few uplifting scriptures, and even tell a joke or two. It was good to see his father smile, though Wick knew his father didn't feel like it. You could always count on him for a good line. His wit was his way of engaging people, making things not as bad as they seemed. He could punctuate a thought or situation better than anyone Wick had ever known.

So, when Grace stood up to leave, she said, "Mr. Watters, I'll be praying for you tonight. Is there anything I can do for you?"

"Yes, ma'am. Please ask him how much longer I have to stay, because I'm ready to go."

Raleigh's fever topped out at 108 degrees that night, no matter how much medicine Charlene administered. Raleigh's vital organs were simply shutting down. Wick was at his bedside when his lifelong hero spent his last breath.

At 2:21 a.m. on Wednesday, November 20, 2013, Raleigh Charles Watters, age eighty-eight, was *content*.

Diane

In 2010, when Wick's sister was just sixty-two years old and before Raleigh passed, Wick's father said something disturbing. "Wick, I'm worried about Diane."

"What do you mean, Daddy?" Wick braced himself.

"She's showing all the signs . . ." Raleigh couldn't finish the sentence. "When she's sitting on the couch where your mother sat, where you are right now, she reads the newspaper, and just like Edith, a little later she'll ask me, 'Did I read today's paper?' Or she'll ask me a question, and not fifteen minutes later ask the same question again.

"I'm afraid she's started down the same road your mother went down," Raleigh finished his thought.

Wick didn't want to think it, much less say the word. He immediately went into denial. "I certainly hope not. Sounds to me like she's getting a little senile."

"At sixty-two?"

"It happens, Daddy. I was reading just the other day that senility can occur in younger people. Dementia isn't necessarily a product of aging, and there are many different forms of it." *I better be careful. I'm spinning a story here that has no legs, just to avoid the "A" word.* "We'll keep an eye on sis."

"Well, okay. We'll have to," Raleigh submitted, though deep down inside both were fearful the nightmare, the curse, could visit upon the Watters family again.

Diane was an industrious woman with a strong work ethic that enabled her to run two businesses in parallel. The landlord of the building she leased built out space to facilitate her enterprises. Wearing two hats, she was an independent insurance agent on one side. When she walked back to and through the common storage room, she entered from the other side into "Diane's Accessories," a popular boutique in the community.

Her insurance sales for high-profile companies earned her trips to domestic venues and Europe, while the boutique fulfilled her dream of ownership. She hired support personnel for both entities.

Blessed with a family of three accomplished children and the same number of grandchildren, Diane was more than content with her world.

However, her dreams were in jeopardy the day a neurologist diagnosed her, at age sixty-four, with early-onset Alzheimer's disease.

Raleigh had been right, of course. He had lived it with Edith and witnessed Diane's behavior firsthand. Wick had feared the inevitability. At least now the entire family knew. They would be called on, either directly or by their own instincts and conscience to help.

Worrisome episodes of trauma, both before and after Diane's diagnosis, were communicated to her neurologist and other doctors, including:

Diane tumbled down a full flight of uncarpeted stairs, leaving her with a gash in her scalp.

Crawling underneath her front porch to retrieve an errant puppy, she lost balance and hit her head on a stone or cement block.

While walking her dog on a leash downtown, Diane's canine pulled her backward, off the curb, for a spill on the asphalt and subsequent blow to the back of her head.

Her husband ostensibly dozing off on the sofa, Diane wandered out the back door and up an elevation to their swimming pool, which had long been covered. She attempted to walk over the cover (now dry-rotted) and fell into the deep end of the empty pool. Their neighbor, in his workshop, heard her screaming and ran over to assist her husband in pulling her out, which they were unable to do. A call was made to 911, and firemen responded, descending into the pool to lift Diane out. Miraculously, she was conscious but had no broken bones, only skin abrasions, contusions, and obviously trauma.

Diane was soon admitted to a long-term-care facility, within its Alzheimer's unit, by her children.

Wick was crushed. The only good thing was that his father had already passed. *Thank God he wasn't here to witness what his daughter was going through.*

Wick's sister was eventually moved to in-home hospice care. The primary nurse termed her condition "accelerated."

Diane literally lay on her death bed. Instructions were given to discontinue any nutrition and administer pain medicine as needed. For seventeen days she lived without any nourishment, just swabs of water pressed on her lips to keep her mouth moist.

Wick visited her bedside for a week, whispered memories in her ear, and painfully watched as his only sibling wasted away, the color in those beautiful brown eyes now faded too.

He held her hand and whispered one last time, "I love you, sis. Please say hello to Mother and Daddy for me."

Diane Watters Grady, seventy-two, died peacefully in her home on Sunday afternoon, October 18, 2020 surrounded by her three children.

Chapter Twenty-Six

Welcome Back

How was the journey with Wick? Now that you have completed it, what is your takeaway? What is your definition of contentment? More specifically, what does it look like for you?

The dictionary defines contentment as "a state of happiness and satisfaction." Simple, but a little more involved than that.

True contentment is totally subjective. Whatever your reasons or seasons, it all comes down to the most important assets in one's life. Those include the following, in no particular order: family, faith, friends, freedom, and fruits of one's labor. Everyone, intentionally or not, prioritizes each according to their station in life and orbit of people with whom they interact. Any one of these assets may ultimately foster one's contentment, but at the end of the day, they are interdependent and essential for optimal contentment.

Wick's path was full of characters like Hollie, Uncle Tom, Reed and Rose, Raleigh and Edith, Uncles Albert and Burton, Coach Stagg, Stan Faulkner, Hank Bremen, Lewis Grizzard, Archie, the Cherokees, Jack Brown, Johnny Harris, and others;

yes, even Sage, who impacted his life. They, too, have their own sense of contentment.

Uncle Tom believed and imparted to Wick that *character* ultimately defines life, and one's *values* and *integrity* are one's wealth.

Wick and I leave you with a simple yet powerful quote (to include women as well):

> "*Remember, no man is a failure who has friends.*"
> —Clarence Odbody, *It's a Wonderful Life*

The End

Acknowledgments

Kudos to Gail Woodard, whose leadership and savvy have been invaluable in steering this book to fruition; and Winsome Lewis, production coordinator, for keeping me between the white lines.

Russell and Erin Marie; Erin Elisabeth and Katie; Avery, Abby, Reece, and Charlotte; Nathan, Noah, and Anna. All for being who you are. Embrace your talents and identify your gifts as you reach for the stars.

Principals Goble and Payne; faculty Evans, Mullis, Johnson, Bridges, Hess, Blalock, Ransom, Frew, Wingard, Presley, Wagner, Wilson, Bentley, Derrick, Long, Green, Nelson, Henderson, Hyatt, Steadman, Lucas, and Jolley. Elementary through high school, they all taught me by the book or by example when public education was all about teaching, not policing and politics. By the way, we all pledged allegiance to the flag, too.

Hubert Lowe, for not firing me on my first day after dumping a full buggy of groceries off the curb. No one told me I was supposed to back it down. That embarrassing moment was a lesson learned.

Georgia Kraft, the paper mill west of town that hired college students in the summers. Some of my best laughs and lessons came from the chemical recovery section of the mill: "Squirmin' Thurman," the only man I ever saw eat a raw onion whole, like an apple, his forehead brimming with sweat as his eyes emptied out tears; Edsel, aka "Wounded Knee," cooking venison medallions in an electric skillet hidden behind the control panel; and Joe Lee, devouring six chili dogs one after the other (he could also yodel, but not at the same time). These were just a few of the characters who added to the experience. If there was room for dessert, Joe Lee and I would take turns cranking the six-quart ice cream freezer, out of sight from tour foremen who rarely made their rounds by the fifth-floor cloistered corner.

While this all sounds like fun, it was temporary. Three seven-story recovery boilers, their beds burning with lava-like smelt (at greater than two thousand degrees), emptied their contents continuously down a single spout off each boiler into a transition tank below. If the spouts were not running, that meant insufficient air was flowing through the boiler and a potential "blackout" was in store. So, every thirty to forty-five minutes, I walked down two flights of steel staircase, then around the boilers with a scaling rod, punching out the buildup inside each air portal. From June through August, the ambient temperature around the boilers varied from 120 to 140 degrees Fahrenheit. The reason I acknowledge that here . . .

Wouldn't you be motivated, anxious, and content to get back to Athens and academia too?

My gratitude to Dan Foster, Henry Freeman, Lewis Grizzard,

and Chuck Perry. Thanks to their influence, I wound up in the right "paper mill."

Gary Shelby, for mentoring me on the business side of publishing.

Dathan and Athaleen Mitchell, for fifteen years of loyalty, opportunity, and growth.

ROFDA CEOs for their twenty years of support: Martin Arter, David Smith, Benny Cooper, George Lankford, Randy Arceneaux, Rich Parkinson, Neal Berube, Bob Obray, Calvin Miller, Craig Burgess, Michael Burgoine, Mike Violette, Gerry Totoritis, Stan Alexander, Hillar Moore, Jay Campbell, Emile Breaux, John Runyan, Randall Simon, Amy Niemetscheck, Jim Ried, Bob Ketchner, Terrell Wooten, Dennis Stewart, David Bullard, Greg Tarr, Dean Sonnenberg, Ray Sprinkle, Al Plamann, James Denges; and Presidents Jim Morton, Ferrell Franklin, and Francis Cameron.

Jesse Garcia, for your unwavering support and friendship. Hope you have your pilot's license now.

Stephanie Reid, for holding all the planes until I could get through security on our barnstorming tour.

Peter Larkin, for your insights and perspectives, whether on industry or Capitol Hill.

Terry Olsen, for your humbling and inspiring letter of October 24, 2001.

Tom Haggai, for your kind letter of August 26, 2011, regarding "the written word."

Finally, veteran Walt Callahan and his relic "Blue Goose" single engine plane, flying me over the City of Seven Hills and Three Rivers as Romulus and Remus took note of my very first flight at seventeen.

Author Ron Johnston and Sage

About the Author

Ron Johnston is a retired president and publisher of B2B magazines that focused on the retail food industry in 48 states. He earned his degree in journalism from the Henry W. Grady School of Journalism at the University of Georgia. In the past, he worked as a sports writer for the *Greenville News* in South Carolina and later for the *Atlanta Journal-Constitution*. Johnston and his wife Harriet, a retired math professor, reside in Braselton and Rome, Georgia.

Made in the USA
Columbia, SC
09 June 2023